The Black Fin Case

by A.T. Weaver and A.M. Burns

Copyright 2016 © MysticHawker Press
http://www.mystichawker.com/

ISBN: 978-1-945632-02-0

Cover design by A. M. Burns
Photo licenses:
www.depositphotos.com 5976209 - © Thye Gn
www.depositphotos.com 116813120 - © Stephane Boussoutroux

Dedicated to:
Sir Halidor Arkellsson – who helped me figure out what Kynth was.

And
Countess Alix Coeurbois – who gave Ken his last name

Chapter One

LONG EERIE shadows cast by the dirty streetlight only added to the darkness in the alley. Bile rose in Detective Greg Williams' throat. The stench of the nearby dumpster in the heat of the late summer night was rancid, and for a moment, he wondered if there was something dead inside. Sweat rolled down his back between the straps of the bulletproof vest. Heart pounding with anticipation, he swallowed hard. It didn't help the thick taste in his mouth dissipate. He pressed his back against the brick wall, and did his best to focus on the situation. He hated drug raids. Even with lots of precautions, there was too much that could go wrong. With a deep breath, he inched slowly toward the dimly-lit window. His partner, John Jackson, followed closely on his heels.

They'd been chasing the Black Fins, a drug gang trying to control Portland's underground, for over six months. The last time he thought the men were cornered, it was like they had known the cops were coming. He hoped this time would be a surprise. Neighbors had reported strange things going on in this house. For the last several weeks, there'd been a lot of people coming and going at all hours.

Three SWAT members approached from the other side of the door. Their protective helmets hid their expressions, but their movements were tense, like springs tightened for action. Everyone's radios were on but silent, like they were supposed to be for a raid. No one had said a word in five minutes while Greg and his men moved into position. The trek down the overly quiet alley had been unnerving. They couldn't hold the lockdown on the neighborhood too long, or the suspects in the house might realize there was something going on. If they were conducting as much business as the neighbors reported, they could notice the lack of traffic, or one of their customers might call to report the blockade set up two blocks around the house in all directions.

Greg reached the window. He shattered it with the butt of his assault rifle and lobbed a tear-gas canister inside. The breaking glass was the loudest thing he'd heard in several minutes; it sounded like an explosion.

Through the hiss of the gas, a television blared with the sound of the latest nonsense politician hooting about immigration. Something was wrong. People should've been running. There should be coughing.

As he feared, another false lead. Greg glanced at Jackson and the SWAT guys. He waited for something to happen. His rifle grew heavy in his grip. A screech rang out in his radio's ear bud.

Greg yanked the earpiece out. "What was that?"

The others did the same, but Jackson's was the only face he could see as the SWAT guys struggled to get their helmets off and earpieces out. Something was wrong, very wrong.

Tires screeched on the alley's filthy asphalt.

Everyone turned toward the sound.

A van raced toward them scattering garbage cans and trash bags. The refuse scattered in the van's wake like dark waves behind a speed boat.

"What the hell?" Jackson asked as he lifted his rifle toward the van.

"Where're the men blocking the alley?" Greg shouted as he copied his partner's move. There shouldn't have been any way for someone to get in or out without going through a police barricade. He reached for his microphone, but bullets started flying. Everything was going to pot and he wasn't sure what he could do about it.

Semi-automatic rifles blazed from the van's windows. Brick and mortar flew in all directions as the bullets struck the wall. The SWAT guys returned fire. Jackson's assault rifle barked loudly several times.

"Get down!" Greg dove for the ground as Jackson spun and fell. He tried to bring his assault rifle around toward the van, but pain erupted in his left leg. He crashed to the ground. His forehead struck the pavement. Rainbow-colored stars swirled in front of his eyes. The rifle fell from his unresponsive hands. Anger surged in him. His head throbbed with pain. The Black Fins had known they were coming. His vision went black as the sound of the SWAT officers' guns overcame the agony in his head. He tried to stay in the game, but it was too much. Greg surrendered to the darkness.

* * *

Greg struggled to open his eyes. He tried to raise his right hand and found it strapped to a board and immobile. Fear lanced through him. He struggled for a moment. The antiseptic odor associated with a hospital room assailed his nostrils. In the distance, voices sounded frantic. Realizing he must be safe, he relaxed. He lifted his left hand and rubbed his eyes. His head ached. What felt like a bandage covered his forehead. A dull pain throbbed in his elevated left leg. Combined with the pounding in his head, it made thoughts hard for Greg to process.

"A-a-a-h." His voice sounded shallow in his own ears.

A soft feminine voice came from somewhere nearby, "Lie still, Detective. I've called for the doctor."

Greg finally got one eye open. "Are all angels as beautiful as you?" He could barely force his voice above a whisper. His throat was dry and scratchy.

"I'm sorry, Detective Williams, you aren't in Heaven." The attractive blonde nurse smiled and adjusted the IV bag attached to a needle in the back of his right hand. "In fact, you'll probably think you're in Hell when the pain meds wear off."

Greg swallowed and ran his tongue around his lips to moisten them. It didn't help much. The inside of his mouth felt like it was full of cotton. He really wanted something to drink. "What happened?" He remembered going in to bring in the Black Fins. The SWAT team was there. There'd been shooting. He suddenly wondered why the rest of the SWAT guys, their backup, hadn't stopped the van when it came toward them. Bullets had been flying from the black van. It got fuzzy after that.

"All I know is you were shot in the leg and hit your head when you fell. I'll let your captain fill you in on the details." She stuck a thermometer in his mouth.

A tall, dark-haired man in a white coat entered the room and took the chart from the nurse. "Good morning. I'm Dr. Davis. How are you feeling?"

The nurse removed the thermometer and looked like she was waiting for the doctor to finish with the chart.

"You tell me." Greg raised his eyebrows, but the bandage on his forehead made the action a little awkward. "Good news first."

After handing the chart back to the nurse, Dr. Davis walked to the side of the bed and shined a light into Greg's eyes. "Well, the good news is, you're alive and fixable. The bad news is, there's a bullet resting against your left femur, and you have a slight concussion."

There was the soft sound of the nurse returning the chart to the foot of the bed. It was beginning to feel rather routine.

Greg lifted his free hand to his head. "How bad?"

The doctor chuckled. "Nothing major on the outside of the head, most of it is on the inside." He pursed his lips. "I doubt its deep enough to scar. After a couple of months it'll just be another line on your forehead."

"Good thing he hit his head." A familiar voice said with a snicker. "I checked to see if it damaged the pavement."

The nurse moved the head of his bed up slightly and then adjusted the pillows behind his head as soon as the doctor moved away from him.

"Funny, Captain," Greg said. He wished they'd bring him something to drink so his throat wouldn't be so scratchy. He wondered what was taking so long in doing that. "What happens next, Doc?"

"We have to remove the bullet. I didn't want to put you under general anesthetic until you woke from the blow to the head. The tests all indicated you should wake today. The swelling's going down nicely. I'll schedule surgery for later today or early tomorrow, depending on operating room availability." He moved to the foot of the bed, lifted the covers, and looked at Greg's leg. "Then there'll be rehab time and physical therapy. How long, I can't say. It'll depend on how things go, but probably a couple of weeks." He retrieved the chart and made some notes before handing it to the nurse. "I'll see you in surgery."

She returned it to the foot of the bed and looked at Greg as the doctor left the room. "Need anything?"

"Some water would be great."

"That should be okay. But, sorry, no food until they schedule surgery though. If it isn't until tomorrow, you'll get some lunch and supper." She turned and strolled out of the room.

"Captain, what happened?" Greg asked after the doctor and nurse left. He was still having trouble talking and wished the nurse would hurry with the water.

Captain Wood stepped quietly over to the side of the bed. "The place was empty. The SWAT guys got off a few rounds at the van, but it got away."

That didn't help explain what had happened to the rest of the SWAT team. "Any injuries besides me?"

"Jackson didn't make it." He grimaced and shook his head. "Bulletproof vests don't cover faces. He took one between the eyes."

"Shit!" Greg rubbed his hand over his face to brush away the sudden tears. His throat tightened, and combined with the dryness in it, he could barely get words past his parched lips. "Over thirty years on the force and two months from retirement. Does Sharon know?" They'd been partners for a long time. Jackson was more of a brother to him than just a partner. He wished he could just go back to sleep for a while and wake up to a different reality, but he was a cop; he knew better. There were no other realities. He was stuck in this one, where gangs killed cops on a regular basis. Greg was lucky he'd escaped with a hole in his leg and a concussion.

"Yeah. I told her myself. She wants to see you, but I asked her to wait." The captain walked to the window and looked out. "They knew you were coming."

"How?" He and Jackson had been so careful who they let in on their information. "We'd spent over a week setting this up. There must be a leak somewhere." That would account for the SWAT guys missing the van coming toward them like it did. But it would also mean a cop was inadvertently responsible for Jackson's death. Greg forced down the anger that suddenly welled up within him, wiping out the grief. He grabbed hold of that anger. He wanted to use it. It could help him focus through getting back on his feet and back on the street. The Black Fins had to pay for what they'd done, and the cop feeding them information was going to pay too. Greg would see to that. "What happened to the guys who were supposed to have blocked off the area?"

Captain Wood turned from the window. "I questioned the captain in charge of them. He said they got an order to stand down from higher up a couple of minutes before the van roared through." He rubbed the back of his neck. "You're a marked man. I think you're really close to busting this thing wide open. You've got somebody very nervous." He shook his head. "I don't think anywhere is going to be safe for you. We lost Jackson, I don't want to lose you too. I've put a guard outside your room."

"Who? If there's a leak, who can we trust?" He'd been with the department fifteen years. He couldn't think of anyone who could be working with any of the gangs, and that meant he couldn't think of anyone he'd really count on to watch out for him. Suddenly the idea of going under the knife became more terrifying. He'd be helpless.

The captain fell silent as the pretty nurse returned with a cup of ice.

"Here you go." She flashed him a soft smile. "Hope this'll help. I couldn't bring water. We got lucky, there's an opening in surgery in a couple of hours, so nothing to eat or drink. The orderlies will be up for you in about an hour. I'll be back with your preliminary pills as soon as they come up from the pharmacy. If you need anything before then, hit the call button." She hurried out of the room.

The captain shut the door behind her, then walked back to Greg's bedside. "Carter's on now. He'll be replaced by Hudson, and then Strader."

"Yeah. I'd trust them with my life." Greg chuckled. The ice made using his voice a lot easier. "I guess I am, aren't I?"

He sighed and laid his head back against the pillows. The three men were ones he'd worked with for years. He knew all three outside of work too. There weren't many others he'd trust with his life more than he did them. All the thoughts of the perils of his own life made him realize he was forgetting someone really important to him. "Would you have someone pick up Casey and take him to the kennel? His vet is Dr. Wilson at Sunnyside Clinic. I don't know how long I'll be away from home."

"No kennel for Casey." The captain smiled. "I'll take him to my house. My boys will love having him. Since their dog died, they've been wanting another one."

"Thanks, Cap." Knowing Casey was safe would make everything else a lot easier for him to endure.

Captain Wood stepped closer to the bed and spoke in a whisper. "When you're out of surgery, I have some plans. They'll take the cooperation of the doctor."

"Like what?" The idea the captain already had a plan, gave Greg a glimmer of hope that they could finally catch the Black Fins and put them out of commission for good.

"I want everyone to think you're hurt worse than you are. I'm putting you on leave. I want the leak to think you're no longer a threat to the organization."

Greg nodded. "In other words, fake it."

The captain flashed him a conspiratory grin. "For all it's worth."

"I can do that." He wondered what the captain was going to be doing while they were faking it. With any luck, by laying a false trail they'd be able to have a little bit of breathing room and get the bad guys to slip up. It would make things a lot easier. To that point, it was like Greg and Jackson had been foxes trying to catch prairie dogs, always too slow to actually grab anyone. Maybe if they thought the cops weren't actually hunting them, some progress could be made, if the captain could find honest cops to put on the situation.

The captain walked toward the door. "I'll check back with you and the doctor later," he said in his normal voice.

Through the open door, Greg heard him talking to Carter as he left. "He's going into surgery in a couple of hours. It doesn't look good. Doc says he'll probably be disabled and may have to use a wheelchair. At the least, he'll walk with a cane the rest of his life. Looks like he'll be delegated to a desk job."

"Whoa!" Carter's deep voice broke slightly. "He won't like that. In his place, I'd probably opt for early retirement."

"Yeah. He's a good detective. I hate to see it happen. I've watched him move up the ranks for over fifteen years."

"But he's luckier than Jackson. He's alive."

"Keep your eyes open. No one, and I mean *no one* beyond medical staff, is allowed in."

"You got it, Captain."

Knowing Carter would watch over him until he was on his way to surgery gave Greg the confidence to try and relax as much as his general pain and discomfort would allow. Just thinking that one or more of the guys on the force could be working against them was enough to set his teeth on edge. Every time he heard about police corruption, he'd always been sure his department was clean. He knew Captain Wood prided himself on having the best group of officers he could, but someone had still managed to slip in a bad cop. The very idea gave Greg chills and made his head hurt worse.

* * *

Greg woke the next morning, as Captain Wood walked into the room. He'd already been awake with the nurses helping him take short painful steps. The painkillers had put him out for a little while and he'd welcomed their embrace.

"How's it going today?" Captain Wood asked as he leaned against the wall just under the television.

"Been better," Greg said, thankful his throat wasn't as dry as it had been the previous day. "But I'll survive."

Captain Wood nodded. "That's good."

Doctor Davis arrived before they could really strike up a conversation. Captain Wood closed the door behind the doctor and moved closer to Greg's bed. Speaking in a low voice so as not to be heard outside of the room, he said, "Doc, I want you to do something for us."

The doctor raised an eyebrow and looked a little dubious. "What's that?"

"I want you to send Williams to re-hab. I'd like for people to think his leg is worse than it is. Think you can do that?"

"He doesn't have local family or people he lives with. He'll be going to rehab anyway." He flashed Greg an apologetic look. "That's just standard procedure." He looked at the captain. "I suppose you have a reason for the other."

"We believe there may be a leak in our department. I want that person to think Greg is unable to work."

The doctor pursed his lips. "I don't like falsifying records, but I'll see what I can do."

Greg remained silent as they worked out the details. He also didn't like the idea of official records being falsified, but knew if there was a mole in the police department there was a good chance there was also one in the hospital. The doctor would need to do a little manipulating of his own if Greg was going to stay safe until he'd be able to defend himself again. He had a lot to pay the Black Fins back for and he'd find the person responsible for killing Jackson and bring them to justice, one way or the other.

Chapter Two

GREG SAT in the sunroom of the rehabilitation facility bored out of his mind and about to go stir crazy after two weeks of watching soap operas, game shows, talk shows, and old sitcom re-runs. Since the place didn't even have open Wi-Fi, he couldn't get any news on his laptop, and the nurses fussed when they caught him with his cell phone out, saying it could potentially interfere with some of the medical equipment. He'd tried unsuccessfully to talk them into letting him have some of his carving tools and a bit of wood to help him fend off the boredom that had become his constant companion, but they were afraid the tools could be used as weapons. Even if it was a way to throw people off his trail, he didn't like being cooped up in the rehab center. There were other people, men and women who had local family who could drive them back and forth from the rehab sessions who didn't have to stay in the damned center. He wanted to be out where he could be working on things.

He looked around. Most of the residents were at least in their sixties or seventies. It made him wonder what his life was going to be like in a few years when he wasn't able to take care of himself. He didn't have any children like most of his friends did. He didn't even have a boyfriend, and he might as well not have any family. Most of the guys he'd gone out with in his early days as a cop didn't like dating someone who could be called out of the house at the drop of a hat. He'd never realized being a gay cop was going to be such a lonely life.

If nothing else, his time in rehab had given him plenty of opportunity for reflection, and he decided he was tired of being alone. He wanted someone to be there for him when he came home from a long shift. Someone to care when he'd had a hard day and could give him more feedback than just a wet tongue on his cheek.

A small Sheltie ran into the room toward him barking excitedly.

"Casey!" Greg leaned over and held out his hands.

The dog jumped into his lap and licked his face.

Greg laughed and hugged him close. "It *is* you. How are you, boy?" He couldn't believe they'd actually let his dog in to see him. Casey was the one thing he missed most with his forced medical incarceration.

Martha Wood strolled into the room followed by her two sons. The boys were spitting images of their father. Martha looked a lot more tired than Greg remembered seeing her. She was several years younger than her husband. The captain had waited until he was in his middle thirties before he found someone to settle down with. Greg was that age, and hoped he could be as lucky in finding a mate.

"Don told me we could visit. We thought you two might like to see each other. I know he's missed you." Her smile was tight but genuine.

Greg hugged the dog close. "No more than I've missed him."

Casey jumped down and sniffed around Greg's chair. He ran between the two boys for a moment as they silently leaned up against the wall across from Greg's chair. That was fairly normal for them. They were both quiet, but observant boys. Greg often teased the captain that he'd been grooming them to be detectives from the time they could walk and talk.

For a second, Casey stood between Greg and the boys, looking from one to the other before he jumped back up and lay down on Greg's lap. The action was a bit jarring to Greg's leg, but didn't hurt as badly as it would've a week earlier. He didn't mind, it was just good to have Casey back, even for a few minutes.

Martha pulled up a chair. "How are things going? Does the doctor say when you'll get out of here?"

"He said yesterday I can go home Monday." He buried his face in Casey's fur, enjoying the smell of dirt and dog. "Won't be too soon for me. Even if I can't walk very far, it's better than sitting in here." He turned to the boys. "How's school going? I know it just started."

Donny, the older boy, shrugged. "It's okay, I guess."

"You're a senior this year, aren't you?" Greg winked at him. "I'll bet you have to beat the girls off with a stick."

As Donny blushed, his freckles faded into the background.

His younger brother grinned and lightly punched his arm.

An elderly woman walked past and glared at Martha.

Greg grinned. "I think you've made my girlfriend jealous," he whispered and winked at Martha.

She chuckled. "I'll let Don know you'll be ready Monday. He'll have someone pick you up." She pulled a notepad and pen from her purse. "Don still has the key to your house. I'll swing by and make sure things are okay and then go by the grocery store and stock up for you. I cleaned out the fridge while you were in the hospital. Didn't want you to come home to fuzzy food. Tell me what you need." She made a list of the things he thought of, then stood, leaned over, and kissed his cheek. "Call Don when the doctor releases you." She snapped her fingers. "Come on, Casey. We have to go."

The dog whined and looked at Greg.

He held Casey close to his chest. "It's okay, boy. You go with Martha and the boys. Have lots of fun. I'll see you in a couple of days." He set him on the floor. He glanced at Donny. "Make sure to get him lots of exercise. I won't be up for tons of time at the park for a while yet."

"I will." Donny nodded slightly as he and his brother pushed off from the wall to stand closer to their mother. "If you want, we can come over after school and play with him." He looked at his mother. "That is if Mom will let us use the car."

"I'm sure we can work something out." She ruffled his hair.

"Mo-om."

Greg smiled. "That would be great." He'd always enjoyed the way the captain's family had begun to feel like an extension of his own. It made him more relaxed and happy.

Casey walked to Martha, then turned and looked back at Greg.

Martha clicked a leash on his collar and led him and the boys out.

Greg watched until they were out of sight, and then wiped his eyes on his sleeve. There were a lot of things he'd been able to forget about for a while as the nurses and physical therapists put him through the torture they called rehab. Walking with the cane had been really tricky and even if the captain hadn't wanted him out of the way for a while, since he didn't have anyone at home, he'd have had to stay in the facility until he could safely get around on his own. They hadn't even let him go to Jackson's funeral. He'd barely seen anyone besides Captain Wood, since he'd been there. Greg was ready to get out and find the person responsible for his shooting and Jackson's death.

* * *

It was all Greg could do not to glare at Stan, the orderly, standing in his door.

"Sorry, Mr. Williams. You know it's time for lights out. You've been here a couple of weeks and should know our schedule."

Greg sighed. "Okay." He closed his laptop, even if he'd been planning on watching *Serenity* after his all afternoon and evening *Firefly* binge. He knew the schedule, but he was getting tired of it. The whole thing was making him feel old. He didn't know how people stood being locked up like this. Again he wished he had someone at home who could have helped him through his convalescence. It would've still been maddening. He never dealt with injury or illness well, but it would be better than being incarcerated like he was.

Stan smiled. The fact he was young and attractive wasn't lost on Greg, but he wasn't in the mood to appreciate beauty. Besides, he knew Stan was straight. He'd met his perky young wife. They made a good-looking couple. He just wanted to go home and get back on the

14

trail of the Black Fins so he could lock them away for everything they'd done.

"If you need anything, just buzz me." The orderly turned off the light, then disappeared down the hall, his soft shoes making weak slaps on the tile as the door slowly closed behind him.

Greg listened to the sound grow further away until the closing door blocked it out completely. He opened his laptop back up, turned the volume down to the point he could barely hear it, and hit play on the disk he'd just put into the player before the man showed up.

The opening credits finished and beeping started in the hallway. Greg hit pause on the movie so he could hear what was going on. The light coming in from under his door went out. Greg closed his laptop and leaned over to put it on the chair next to his bed. Something was going on. He felt around for his cane. It leaned against the chair. In his time in the facility, he'd grown accustomed to it in his hand. He leaned on it and his injured leg didn't complain as much as he slid out of bed and headed for the door.

Chaos poured out of the darkness when Greg opened the door.

"What's going on?" yelled the older woman next door.

"We're working on getting it fixed!" the orderly shouted. "Please stay in your rooms."

Greg wished he could see, but the building was completely dark. He couldn't even see any flashlights. An idea hit him, and he turned back toward his night stand. His smart phone had a flashlight app. At that point he didn't care if the facility didn't want him using the phone; he might save a life or two. The thought of being able to help bolstered Greg's sagging spirits. He felt like he was back in action.

It was harder than he thought it would be to find the night stand in the dark. As he opened the drawer, his door opened. A flashlight beam passed over him and Greg froze.

"You're supposed to be in bed, asleep," said a raspy voice. "This would be easier that way."

Greg's hand tightened on his cane. "Sorry, but I don't ever make things easier." He spun toward the voice. The flashlight shone in his eyes, blinding him. He swung the cane. It connected with a satisfying crack.

"Damn." The man stumbled away, the flashlight fell to the floor.

Moving as fast as his injured leg would allow, Greg pounced on the flashlight. He got his hand on it, just as a heavy boot crashed into his fingers.

With his other hand, Greg swung the cane again. It cracked into the man's shin and the man hobbled back a couple of steps.

"Fucking cop." The man kicked at Greg as Greg managed to get hold of the flashlight again. It was a big metal one, like the police used. He'd been taught in the academy how to use one as a weapon. He swung it hard up into his attacker's groin. It connected with a pleasing soft crunch.

"Damn it!" The man turned and hobbled from the room.

Greg turned the flashlight in the direction he'd gone and struggled to get to his feet. He wasn't sure why the man hadn't been shooting at him. Maybe he'd thought he'd smother Greg with a pillow while he slept. It was yet another question to add to the ones already piling up. He hobbled as fast as he could into the hallway.

"Hey, get back to your room!" Stan shouted.

"Fuck you!" the man replied.

"You're not one of my patients," Stan objected.

"Stan, get out of here!" Greg shouted. "He just tried to kill me."

"What?" Stan's question was cut off with a gurgling sound.

Greg shown the light in the direction of Stan's voice. His attacker had an arm wrapped around Stan's throat. Stan was clawing ineffectively at him.

"Back off, cop," the man said in a dangerous growl. "I will kill him. You don't want that on your conscience do you?"

Greg didn't want anyone hurt because of him. He'd lost Jackson, he didn't want to lose Stan too. No matter how much the orderly pissed him off, he and his wife were expecting their first child any day now. "Okay. Let Stan go. He hasn't done anything to you."

The Black Fin Case

Stan stomped hard on the man's foot, then kicked the same shin Greg had whacked with the cane. The man shoved Stan toward Greg and stumbled toward the central room that looked out over the river. He picked up a chair and threw it out the window that shattered, sending shards of glass toward the water below the building.

"What in the hell?" Greg took three quick steps toward the man, then his injured leg collapsed under him. Greg hit the floor as the man jumped out of the window. It was a three-story fall. Seconds later, a loud splash sounded as Greg lay on the floor, trying not to complain about the pain in his leg, and hoping his adventure wasn't going to slow him getting out of the facility the next day. But he'd just proved it wasn't safe for him to be there. The captain would understand and get him out as fast as possible.

* * *

Greg leaned on his cane as he walked into his living room. He wasn't sure he'd ever get used to having to use a cane all the time, even if it was just a ruse, and hoped he'd soon be able to set it aside. But cane or no, he felt good about being out of all medical areas and back somewhere that was familiar and comforting. A place that smelled lived in and not so sterile. "It's good to be home. Thanks for the ride, Carter." After the attempt on his life the previous night, he was happier than ever to be somewhere he knew where everything was, and he'd be able to have his gun again.

"No problem." Carter set Greg's suitcase next to the sofa. He'd seemed at a loss for words on the whole drive from the rehab center to Greg's house. "It's good to see you back on your feet, even if you do have a third leg there."

"How about a beer?" Greg headed for the kitchen. He suddenly didn't want Carter to leave quickly. It would be nice to sit and actually talk to someone under the age of sixty, other than the nurses at the rehab, for a little while. "I think the captain's wife put some in the fridge."

"I'll get it." Carter hurried past Greg, heading into the kitchen.

17

"Hey, don't let this cane fool you. I may be slow, but I can get around." Greg grinned. Just being home made him feel better. "After all, it's my house, and I'm the host. Sit down."

The doorbell rang.

Carter continued toward the kitchen. "I'll get the beer. You answer the door."

Inwardly, he was thankful he hadn't gotten all the way to the kitchen as he turned and hobbled back the way he'd come. Greg opened the door and Casey ran in followed by Captain Wood.

"Hey, Casey." Greg bent over and petted the frantic sheltie. Casey gave him a couple of quick licks in return. "We're home."

Wood unsnapped the leash, and the dog ran around the room sniffing every piece of furniture. He acted like he needed to make sure everything was just as he'd left it.

"Carter, make that three beers. Have a seat, Captain." Greg settled on the couch.

Captain Wood sat in a chair facing him. "I talked to your doctor. He said you need to take it easy for a while." He motioned toward the kitchen with his head and winked. "You have some vacation coming. Take it."

"And do what?" Greg didn't bother trying to hide his irritation at the order even though he knew it was for Carter's sake. He'd been hoping to hit the streets running...so to speak, and get busy on finding the Black Fins...and more importantly the departmental problem. "I'd rather be busy."

Casey jumped up beside him and snuggled close to his good leg. His tail never stopped moving, even as he settled his muzzle on Greg's knee. It made things all the better. He hadn't realized how much he missed the little things like Casey's head on his leg.

Greg stroked the dog's head, giving him scratches behind the ears. It was good to be home with Casey by his side. He'd missed the companionship. He again wondered what it would be like if he had someone human to come home to.

The Black Fin Case

Carter came back into the room with the beers and set them on the coffee table. "Be right back."

The captain picked up a beer and took a drink. He gave a slight smile, a look Greg recognized as his appreciation for the beer. He'd always thought the captain was fairly easy to read for a policeman, but he knew the man well enough to know not everything he thought or felt ended up on his face.

"I can't have you out in the field as long as the Black Fins are hunting you. If you come in, you'll be stuck behind a desk."

Greg waved his arm around. "Better there than stuck here." Even though he was happy to be home, if he was confined there, it would get to be as bad as the rehab center had been.

Carter returned with a tray of crackers, cheese, and sliced sausage. "Captain, your wife sure knows how to stock a fridge."

He set the tray down, picked up a beer, and sat on the other side of Casey. "The captain's right, Williams. You should take some time off. Go fishing. Or better yet, find a good-looking woman." He rubbed the dog's ears.

Greg picked up a cracker and a piece of cheese. "Sorry, Carter, you know I don't swing that way." He'd been out at work for years, but so many of his coworkers still assumed he was straight. He was a big masculine cop. He wasn't supposed to like men, but he didn't have much of a choice; it was how he was wired.

Carter chuckled and blushed. "So, okay, find a hot man."

* * *

After the guys left, Greg took Casey and a beer out in the back yard and sat on the patio.

"What do you think, Case? Should we take a vacation? I know I need to call someone to come cut the grass. I don't think this leg will let me do it for at least a couple more weeks." He picked up a tennis ball and threw it for Casey to chase. The dog hunted around in the tall grass before finding the ball and returning. He knew some people would think he was crazy talking to a dog, but it often helped alleviate the loneliness. "Maybe Donny will do the mowing when he comes to play with you." There were a few things he wasn't going to be able to do, but he didn't want to let his physical changes stop him completely. He'd go on and get back to the active man he'd always been. Besides, if he let himself go, just because he wasn't able to get around as well as he had been in the past, he wouldn't be able to find a hot guy to eventually settle down with. If he survived the gang long enough to do that.

Casey came and lay at his feet. For a while everything seemed like it had for the past few years. It felt right and normal.

Chapter Three

GREG HAD just eased himself down into his recliner and started to reach for his turkey sandwich when the doorbell rang. Casey raised his head from his paws, but didn't go running to the door barking. That meant it was someone they knew. Casey was always prepared to bark like a mad thing whenever a pizza delivery guy stopped by, or worse, when there was a new postman.

Trying to ignore the pain in his leg, Greg stood and walked to the door. His motion-sensitive porch light had come on and illuminated the drawn face of Sharon Jackson. Greg threw the door open.

"Sharon." He enfolded her in his arms. "Oh, God." His throat tightened and his knees threatened to buckle under him as she hugged him back.

For several minutes the two of them stood in the doorway hugging as tears flowed down their faces. In that moment, Greg realized he hadn't really expressed his grief at Jackson's loss. It was all so fresh, but holding Sharon, it all poured out. Somehow her being there made everything that much more real. Jackson was never coming back. They both were left with huge holes in their lives, places in their souls that would never be filled by anyone.

As their tears slowed, Greg noticed Casey pushing against his legs, and stepped back into the house, so he could close the door.

"Oh, Greg." Sharon sniffled and fished around in the purse slung over her shoulder. She pulled out a handful of tissues and blew her nose. "I'm sorry. I hadn't meant to fall apart like that." She blew her nose again. "I've been holding together so well."

Greg took her hand and led her to the couch. "It's okay. I know how you feel. It's been rough." He flashed back to all the times she and Jackson had come over for various things. She normally had a baked dish of some sort with her, even when it wasn't a party. She was always concerned that he wasn't eating right. Her empty hands looked wrong, as much as her not having Jackson at her side.

She shook her head and sat demurely on the couch. "I just couldn't believe it when Captain Wood showed up at the house. He said John had been killed and you were in the hospital." She stared at her hands as she balled the tissues tight. "I'm sorry I didn't come see you in the hospital. It was all happening so fast. So much."

"Don't worry about it." Greg put his arm across her shoulders and drew her against him. She was a fairly dainty woman and the few times he'd hugged her, he was always afraid he was going to break her. "I understand. Honestly, I haven't been much up for company."

She nodded. "Me too." She gave him a weak smile. "But there have been so many people around me. Like they were afraid to leave me alone. The kids all finally left yesterday. Sally hadn't visited in almost five years. They were stationed overseas when James died. She got here the day after the raid. That's the reason I didn't come to see you in the rehab. John's death really hit her hard. She wanted me to go back east with her." Sharon brushed her hair back from her face. "But this is my home. James and John are buried here."

"John's death hit all of us." Greg swallowed hard. His tears were still very close to the surface, but he didn't want to lose it again with Sharon. He wanted to be strong for her. "He was there when I joined the department, and he took me under his wing. I learned a lot from him, things they don't teach in the academy."

The Black Fin Case

Sharon kept nodding. "I'm sorry you missed the service. It was very nice. They gave me a folded flag. John Jr. went and got a frame for it, but I can't bring myself to hang it over his favorite chair." Her hand on the tissue tightened to the point liquid dripped from her hand onto the carpet. "I got a stupid flag, Greg. They took my John and all I got back was a stupid flag." Her voice cracked and she shook. "It was just two years ago we lost James." Anger colored her voice. "John blamed the Black Fins for his death. He believed it was their drugs he got hooked on and overdosed. He was so happy six months ago when you two finally got assigned to their case, and now this."

Greg held her tight as her tears started again. He did his best to rein his in, but water still moistened his face. "I know, Sharon. It's not right. That's why John and I were trying so hard to get them." He suddenly wondered who his flag would go to if he got killed in the line of duty. He didn't have any family left alive except his homophobic older brother in Chicago. He hadn't seen or heard from Mike since their grandmother's funeral six years earlier. Mike and his fundamentalist wife had made it plain then that they wanted nothing more to do with him. He was gay and a cop, a double hit against him in both their minds. Mike had always blamed the police department for their parents' deaths. He'd been five and Mike ten when their father died in the line of duty and their mother killed herself a week later. Their maternal grandparents had taken the boys in and reared them.

When Sharon's tears dried a second time, she pulled out another tissue, blew her nose again, and took a deep breath. "I'm sorry, Greg. I didn't come over here to just cry on your shoulder. God knows I've done my share of crying since John died."

"And don't feel bad about that," Greg said, keeping a tight embrace on her shoulders. "You've got to take your time. John was the main focus of your life for close to forty years."

"Yet it seems like just yesterday I met him." She sighed and got a sad, faraway look. "Did he ever tell you we met when he was putting a ticket on my car?"

Greg chuckled. It had been one of Jackson's favorite stories. "Many times. It was his first day on traffic detail."

"And I was parked in front of a fire hydrant so I could run into the bank." A soft grin broke her frown. "I pleaded with him to be nice to me, and he said I'd have to go out with him. I guess today that would be considered police abuse of power, or sexual harassment, or something like that. I was just happy to agree. He was very handsome in his uniform."

"And he always said you were the prettiest woman he ever gave a ticket to, or I should say, tried to ticket." Greg wished he had someone like Jackson had Sharon.

"He always told me that too." She blew her nose again, then shoved the tissues into her purse. "What are we going to do, Greg?"

He shrugged. "I'm going to find the Black Fins and make them pay for what they did to John and James."

Sharon nodded. "Good. Get in a few licks for yourself too. You got really banged up."

"Yeah." Greg touched his leg. "But this will heal."

Casey came over and put his head between them with a soft whimper.

Sharon scratched his ears. "It's okay, Casey. If anything ever happens to Greg, I'll take care of you. You're a good dog."

"Yes, he is." Greg leaned back on the couch. He didn't want to be put on desk detail. He wanted to be out on the streets digging until he figured out who had betrayed them. He owed Jackson and Sharon that much. It would be a lot better to give her the closure of knowing her husband's killers were off the streets and not likely to make more widows and orphans. He just didn't know who he could trust while he worked on the case.

Their conversation dissolved into catching up. She wanted to know how long Greg was going to be down. She assured him she was going to be okay, no matter how wet she'd gotten his shoulders during her visit. It was nearly two hours later when she pulled herself together enough to leave, and Greg was able to return to his sandwich.

* * *

The Black Fin Case

The shrill beeping of the smoke alarm and Casey's barking roused Greg from a deep sleep. It had felt so good to fall asleep in his own bed, it took a minute to realize something was happening.

He sat up and slung his legs over the side of the bed. "Casey, what's wrong with you? It's the middle of the night. Do you have to go out?" He patted the bed and Casey came trotting over to him, then turned and growled at the closed bedroom door.

Then he smelled it. *Smoke.*

His stomach clenched as he registered the "beep, beep, beep" of the smoke alarm. Flipping the bedside light on, he scrambled for his jeans.

Black tendrils seeped under the bedroom door.

Sirens wailed in the distance.

He jerked his jeans on, fumbling slightly with the stiffness of his leg. Then Greg slipped his feet halfway into his tennis shoes, grabbed his gun and wallet from the stand, pulled his grandmother's quilt off the bed, and flung it over his shoulder. He wanted to save the quilt, it was the last thing he had of his grandmother. He wasn't about to leave it to a fire if he could help it.

He opened the window, picked up a chair, and smashed through the screen.

The sirens screamed louder as firetrucks turned the corner.

"Come here, Casey." He scooped the dog up in his arms and lifted him through the window. In his hurry, he was glad Casey didn't struggle against being picked up like he did sometimes. "It's a good thing we're on the ground floor."

A shot rang out as he dropped the dog onto the yard.

Casey yelped.

The night in the alley came rushing back. He couldn't stand the thought of losing Casey the way he'd lost Jackson. "Casey!" Greg pulled his gun from his waistband. "You son-of-a-bitch! You shot my dog!"

He emptied his clip in the direction of the shot, and then crawled out the window and dove toward the ground leaving his shoes behind.

Greg screamed as his knees buckled under him, and sharp pain erupted in his leg. He lay there on the ground, trying to get the strength to crawl over to Casey as the emergency lights cast their kaleidoscope of colors around the yard, making it hard to see.

A man ran toward him and he raised his empty gun.

The man stopped and held up his hands in the universal sign of surrender. "Don't shoot! I'm a fireman."

Casey's whines carried through the pain as Greg tried to get up. "Someone shot my dog. Take care of him first."

"Just lie still." The fireman put a hand on his shoulder, trying to hold him still. "We got to him first. A paramedic is already checking him over."

Greg dropped his gun as the adrenaline faded and the pain in his knee dropped him into darkness.

* * *

Sunlight streamed through the hospital window.

Greg opened his eyes, lifted the covers, and saw his bandaged knee. He didn't feel much pain even though it had hurt like hell when he landed on it. An IV in his left arm led to a meter dispensing drugs.

He turned his head and saw one of the nurses who'd taken care of him previously.

"Good morning, Alice." He grinned. "We have to stop meeting like this."

"Good morning, Detective." She picked up his arm and placed her fingers on his wrist. "I didn't expect to find you here when I came in this morning."

Greg tried to sit up. The pain hit harder and his head swam.

Alice pushed against his shoulder, forcing him back without a lot of effort. "Lie still, Detective."

He didn't want to do that. The last time he'd woken up in the hospital, it had been to find out Jackson was dead. He had to know Casey was all right. Greg didn't want to just lie still. "Find out about my dog, would you please? I think he got shot last night."

The Black Fin Case

Captain Wood hurried into the room as he spoke. "Casey's okay. The bullet just grazed his shoulder and got stuck in his fur. He didn't even need a bandage or to have the shoulder shaved. He's at my house again." He chuckled. "Donny's decided this is good practice since he wants to be a vet."

Dr. Davis came in. "When I told you it was okay to resume normal activity, I didn't mean jumping out of windows." He grinned crookedly.

Greg hadn't planned on being that physical either. He chuckled. "It seemed like the best alternative at the time, Doc." He pointed to his leg. "How bad is it this time?"

"Nothing broken. You sprained your knee. No need for surgery, but you'll have to wear a knee brace for a few weeks. You'll be here for a day or two, but should be good to go after that."

Greg tilted his head. "Just keep those good drugs coming." He suddenly wanted to be lost in a haze for a while so he wouldn't have to face the reality of what his life was becoming. He knew the risks of being a cop, but they were all coming home to roost too fast and he wanted to forget at least for a day or so. Casey was safe; that's what mattered most.

The doctor chuckled, and he and Alice left.

* * *

When next he woke, it was with a clear head. Captain Wood was staring out the window, looking over the city. His hands were clasped behind his back and his forefinger tapped a nervous rhythm on his wrist.

Greg ran his free hand through his hair, almost afraid to interrupt the captain's musings. "Captain, they burned my house and shot my dog." He was glad Casey was okay. It would have hurt like hell to lose him; they'd been together since Casey was a puppy, nearly five years.

"I know." The captain didn't turn around, he kept his gaze out the window. "You're a marked man, and we still haven't figured out the leak. I'm putting the same three guards on you while you're here, and no visitors."

"Okay." Greg sighed and wished they could figure it out quickly, but sometimes moles took forever to dig out. He'd read more than a few cases where they were never found. He wasn't sure how long he'd last if they didn't find this one. "Just take care of Casey."

After a couple of quick promises, the captain left.

Before Greg had a chance to reach for the television remote to try to find something at least remotely interesting on, Alice strolled briskly back into the room. "Okay, Detective, the doctor wants you to sit up in a chair for a while. I'll help you up so I can change the bed."

"Can I go to the restroom?" He hadn't wanted to ask the captain to help get him there, even though he'd woken up with the need to go. Luckily it hadn't been overly urgent.

"Sure." She pushed his bedside table out of the way to open a path to the bathroom, then offered him her hands. "Lean on me, and I'll help you to the door."

He cautiously swung his legs over the bed and put his weight on his good knee.

Alice stood on his left, and he put his arm around her shoulder. They moved toward the bathroom door. He grabbed his cell phone off the bedside table as they hobbled past.

He grinned as he pulled the IV rack with him. "You know, if I were straight, I might hit on you."

She snickered. "I don't think my husband would like that."

Greg entered the restroom.

"Here's a cane to use." Alice handed him the implement. "Don't lock the door in case you fall, Detective."

He took the cane. It didn't have the same feel as the one he'd been using for the past month. The idea that his old cane was feeling familiar made Greg a little depressed. He was too young to get attached to something like a cane. "Okay. But don't you think we know each other enough for you to call me Greg?"

"I'll try,"—she grinned—"but I like saying 'detective'."

He held the cane up and looked at it. It was different from the one he'd had before. It didn't have the ergonomic design the other had. "I guess the other one probably got burned up along with the rest of my stuff."

She tilted her head and smiled at him. "But you and your dog are alive."

He nodded. "Yeah. That's something."

Ten minutes later Greg came out of the bathroom and sat in the chair. Once he'd gotten in there, he realized he needed to do a lot more than pee. He'd also checked his phone for any messages or news.

Alice put the finishing touches on the bed and turned to go. "Don't try to get back into bed alone." She handed him the buzzer. "Ring for someone first."

Greg saluted. "Aye, aye, Captain." He set the buzzer on the arm of the chair.

She screwed up her face and shook her head. She took a moment and shot something into his IV drip. "This'll take the edge off the pain. You'll have a few minutes before it kicks in. Then she started for the door. "I'll be back later."

Diving out the window returned to him and he had to know. "Would you please check on something for me?"

She stopped in the doorway. "Sure. What do you need?"

"I think I had a quilt around me when I jumped. Could you see what happened to it?" His throat tightened and his eyes misted over. That quilt really meant a lot to him and he hated the idea of never seeing it again. "It was one my grandmother made when I graduated high school."

She smiled sadly as she turned and left the room. "I'll see what I can find."

Greg wanted to feel a few things out before the drugs kicked in again. He sat and looked toward the door. "Hey, Carter, are you out there?"

"Nope." Officer Kyle Hudson stuck his head in the door. "You got me for now."

"Come in and talk to me." Greg gestured toward the vacant chair that faced the door and the bed.

With pursed lips, Hudson shook his head. "Captain's orders are to guard the door."

Greg cocked his head and tried to look pathetic, hoping to garner some sympathy. "You can do that from in here."

Hudson did as Greg suggested and sat watching the doorway.

"Tell me, Kyle, who do you think the leak is?" Not being sure exactly how much time he'd have, Greg cut to the chase.

"No idea, Greg." Hudson rubbed his chin thoughtfully. "I'd like to think you and the captain are wrong about this, but the signs say you're right. I just can't believe anyone in the precinct would be involved with this."

"I guess it'll probably be up to you and the rest of the good guys to find the bad one. Looks like I'm out of it." He hated admitting that to anyone, but he didn't want to do anything to put others at risk. The best option he could think of was taking his vacation. Maybe with a bit of distance the Black Fins would back off, and he could dig up things via the internet. And if he couldn't find something, maybe Captain Wood could. There had to be a trail of something he could track. If there was a mole, he, or she, might have money coming in from some place. Greg sighed and his thoughts slowed as his painkillers kicked in again. They hit harder than Alice suggested they would. They were doing more than just taking the edge off.

* * *

The next morning, Greg was sitting on the chair after breakfast. He broke into a smile as Alice came into his room carrying his grandmother's quilt. "You found it."

"The paramedics had it downstairs in one of the lockers where they keep stuff they find." She held it out to him. "I took it home and washed it for you."

He took the quilt and held it to his chest. It didn't smell right; she hadn't used the same detergent as he did, but it felt perfect. The quilt was safe. For several seconds his throat and chest were so tight he wasn't sure he could speak. "Like I said before, you're an angel. I hope your husband appreciates what he has."

"He does." She grinned and winked. "We've been married over twenty years."

"Do you have kids?"

She stuck a thermometer in his mouth and took his wrist between her thumb and fingers. "Two boys and a girl; and one grandbaby."

She removed the thermometer and picked up the chart from the foot of the bed.

Greg raised his eyebrows. "You certainly don't look old enough to be a grandmother."

"Thanks." She made some notes on the chart and hung it back. "Like I said yesterday, don't try to get back into bed by yourself. Ring for help."

Greg relaxed in his chair as she walked out. He felt a little silly hugging the quilt so tightly, but it was one of his most treasured belongings. He'd lost the house, but he still had the quilt, Casey, and his life. Somehow he'd find the people responsible and make them pay. Even after washing, there was still the lingering smell of smoke on the quilt. It would help him focus on what he had to do.

Chapter Four

TWO WEEKS later, Greg walked into the precinct room. He'd tried everything he could think of to track down the leak from his computer in his motel room and still had no leads. Everyone looked squeaky clean. It was more maddening than anything he'd ever done before. He couldn't believe it was happening. There had to be some trace of something somewhere. He couldn't find it, and so far, the captain hadn't found it either.

His normally neat hair hung in oily strings. He liked his hair long, but it was a good three inches longer than usual. A week-old beard shadowed his usually clean-shaven jaw. His good knee stuck out of a hole in his dirty, second-hand jeans. He limped and leaned heavily on the cane in his left hand. A brace encased his left knee. He knew he looked horrible, but he didn't care. His life was crap and he was ready to make a major change.

Officer Nancy Whitaker looked at him. "Damn, Williams! You look like shit."

"You try getting shot and having your partner killed and see how you look," he growled. He instantly felt a twinge of guilt for going at her, but he'd been snapping at everyone for a while and if he was going to go through with the captain's plan, he didn't need any positive emotions trying to stop him. "And if that wasn't enough, they tried to kill me in the rehab, burned my house, and shot my dog."

"Williams," Captain Wood bellowed as he stomped out of his office. "What are you doing here? The doctor hasn't released you for duty yet."

Greg ran his free hand through his unkept hair. "Sorry, Captain. I got stir crazy."

The captain walked over to him. "Whitaker's right. You look like shit. Couldn't you at least shampoo that mop on your head and shave?"

Greg laid his badge, gun, and an envelope on Whitaker's desk. "I quit." He'd said it. He hoped everyone believed him. He needed breathing room to think, plan, and probe. Since he hadn't found anything new, he still wasn't sure who he could trust.

The captain's eyes widened in surprise. "What do you mean?"

"I mean, I'm through! I can't walk. They tried to kill me. Then they burned my house and shot Casey. I give up." He'd been trying to convince himself that he could go back to being a cop, but if he couldn't even track down one bad police officer from his motel room with full access to the precinct's systems, what good was he going to be on a desk job? It was time for him to get out and find something new to do. He knew his actions were just a ruse, but he had to play everything over in his head to keep things as real as he could make them. He had to be convincing; if he wasn't, he might not throw the Black Fins' leak off his trail.

Staring at the items on the desk, Captain Wood shook his head. "Look, Greg, I know it's rough, but the doctor says your leg will get better, Casey was just scratched, you got a new car which is better than that wreck you were driving, and your house was insured."

"That house belonged to my grandparents. I was practically raised in it." Greg was thankful he was mad, it kept him from tearing up when he talked about the house and his grandparents. If he broke down, it would all go to hell, and he'd never pull anything off.

"Yes, the house was full of memories and keepsakes that you'll never replace, but you and Casey are alive. That's the main point. Come on in my office and we'll talk." The captain put his hand on Greg's shoulder. They walked slowly the short distance from Whitaker's desk to the captain's office. It felt like every eye in the office was on Greg until the captain closed the door behind him He hoped everyone was enjoying their show.

"Take some time off." The captain went behind his desk and reached into one of the drawers. "I've approved six months' leave for you. You have that much time coming in vacation since you never take any."

He handed Greg an envelope. "Here's the approval plus your vacation pay. Take Casey, find a sandy beach somewhere, and just relax. You're too good a cop to give up."

Greg took the envelope and shook it. "I'll think about it. Six months is a long time." He wished they could drop the ruse, but the captain had said he'd been over his office several times, and it was bugged repeatedly. Time away was to give him an opportunity to actually find something useful. That would go a long way to giving him back his sense of dignity and purpose.

He walked out of the captain's office and toward the front door. He stopped in the threshold, and turned back. "Keep up the good fight, guys," he said and saluted his fellow officers. He didn't wait to see if any of them saluted back. He didn't want a big emotional display. He turned and hurried down the steps and toward his waiting car.

Back at his motel room, Greg opened the envelope. "Wow, Casey. This check will keep us fed for a long time."

A note lay next to the check. He read it silently.
Paco's Tacos, 6 o'clock.

Chapter Five

GREG LIMPED into Paco's Tacos leaning on his cane. Although he wore the same jeans with the hole in the knee, they had been washed, and he'd showered, shaved, and shampooed his hair. He hadn't, however, gotten a haircut.

Captain Wood and Martha sat on one side of a booth toward the back of the café.

Greg slid in across the table from them. He smiled at Martha, almost ignoring the captain. "Good evening, Martha. You're looking good tonight."

"Thank you, Greg." She smiled back. "I'm glad to see you up and around. The boys were sorry to send Casey back home."

"I really appreciate all they did. I'll have to find some way to thank them." He drummed his fingers on the tile table top for a moment. "Maybe a new video game?"

She chuckled. "They'd like that, but you don't need to pay them."

"I must say, you look a bit better than earlier," the captain said, drawing Greg's attention to him.

"You told me to get cleaned up. Sorry I don't have a very large wardrobe right now. Everything burned up in the fire. And I hate hobbling through stores on this cane. It makes shopping damned inconvenient."

The waitress came and took their orders.

The captain turned to his wife. "I think you need to powder your nose, dear." He made a gentle shooing motion with his hands.

"Is it shiny?" She grinned at Greg. "I'll be back."

Greg stood as she left. It was something he'd done all his life when a woman left the table or room. His grandmother had always told him it was just good manners.

"See, Don, some of your men know how to be gentlemen." She walked toward the restroom sign.

"What's the plan?" Greg asked as he resumed his seat. "And don't tell me to find a beach somewhere. You know I don't like hot weather."

They fell silent as the waitress brought their drinks.

The captain continued, once she'd moved out of earshot, "I know. That's why I'm sending you to the woods."

Greg opened his straw and placed it in his glass. "Why do I have to go anywhere?" He sipped his soda.

Captain Wood frowned. "Greg, we've worked together a long time. Ever since you got out of the academy. You're a good cop, and we've become friends in that time. We went over this. There's a hit out on you. I don't want to get a call that you've been shot again or had your car blown up."

"What do you have in mind?" He took another sip of soda. He wasn't sure getting out of town would help his search any more than staying in town was doing. But then again, it might not hurt. It might give the bad guys the idea he'd given up and they might slip up.

"I have a cousin who has a cabin up near Mt. Hood. It's very isolated. Miles from town, and only one other cabin anywhere near."

"And this is supposed to keep me safe? Miles from any help if something happens?" The way his luck was going he wouldn't have internet access or any real way to hunt the Black Fins down. He wasn't sure about spending the winter in the mountains. He liked cold, but several feet of snow on the ground was another matter.

The Black Fin Case

The captain handed him a cell phone. It was a basic flip phone with nothing fancy on it. "This is a burner. I'm the only one who has the number." He dialed from another, identical phone. "This is also a burner. Don't answer that phone unless the call comes from here." Greg's phone rang. He flipped it open and looked at the number. Then the captain handed him a piece of paper and an envelope. "That's a new email on my personal laptop. You're the only one who knows about it. I want you to set up a dummy email and send it to me. Don't use this account for anything else."

Greg stuck the paper into his jeans pocket and laid the envelope on the table. If he was getting a new email, that must mean there was web connection at the cabin. That would make things easier. "So when do I leave? I'll need to get supplies."

"You won't need much. Everything you need will be at the cabin." He grinned. "Although, I'd suggest taking a lot of books and some DVDs with you. I'll get you some stuff. I'm sure the boys have some movies you'd like. If you're seen doing it, folks might wonder why you're buying entertainment before leaving for the beach. TV and internet reception are often spotty. It's satellite, so weather can play havoc with it, but it's gotten better the past few years. About nine miles before you get to the lake, there's a small town called Government Camp. There're a couple of grocery stores, a few restaurants, and a ski shop, though I doubt if you'll be doing much skiing. However, when the snow comes in, it might be difficult to get out to town."

Greg glared at him. "What about clothes? Like I said, I'm kind of low right now."

"Bob's taking a couple of suitcases full of clothes, boots, a heavy coat, and lots of food out to the cabin tomorrow. I checked sizes on the extra clothes in your locker." The captain paused and took a drink from his soda. "I want you to act like you're going to that beach. Shop for swimwear and light-weight clothing. You have a ticket on a flight out of here tomorrow afternoon, but you won't be on it. Carter will. He'll drive your car, park it at the airport, and fly to San Francisco with a dog that looks like Casey. He'll catch a bus out of the airport, rent a car under an assumed name, and return to Portland."

"Where will you get the dog, and what happens to it?" Greg asked gruffly. This was part of the plan that was hitting him wrong. Dogs were innocents and didn't deserved to be used and discarded. "You aren't just abandoning it?"

"Don't worry. It's a dog from a no-kill shelter, and will come back with Carter." The captain chuckled. "It's at my house right now. Donny's been wanting a dog like Casey so it'll probably end up back at my house permanently."

Greg grinned. "Okay. Just want to make sure it's all right."

"I hope anyone who tries to track you will find a dead end at San Francisco."

"If Carter has my car, what am I supposed to drive?"

"Carter will show up at your motel to trade cars with you. He's the only one who knows what's going on. He and I talked things over away from the office so no one could overhear us. I trust him. I'm betting both our lives on him being clean."

Martha returned to the table. "How is the leg, Greg?"

"The doc says I'm lucky to be walking at all." He patted the brace on his leg. "Without this brace and cane, I'd be stuck in a chair."

The waitress brought their meals. It all smelled great and the sizzle from the plates made Greg's mouth water.

Greg opened the envelope. Inside was a pre-paid Visa card and a note with the phone number of the burner phone. He laid it down and took a bite of his tamale spread.

Don tapped the card with the handle of his fork. "This card has a $5,000 balance. You shouldn't need any more than that where you're going. If you do, call me on the burner phone. You don't need to spend all the vacation money I gave you, unless you just want to."

Greg nodded and slipped the card into his wallet. He still wasn't sure how this was going to turn out, but he was going to go along with it.

Chapter Six

THE NEXT afternoon, Greg again walked into the squad room. This time, he brought Casey along with him. His jeans, flowered shirt, and straw hat looked brand new, and he'd had a haircut. Overall, he not only looked like the old Greg, he looked like he was about to get on a plane to the beach.

"Well, boys and girls, keep the peace while I'm gone. Casey and I are headed for sunny Hawaii."

Whitaker smiled at him. "I must say you're looking more like yourself."

He sat on the corner of her desk and nodded his head toward his a few feet from hers. There was a man sitting there he didn't recognize, and also a new face at Jackson's desk. "I see I've been replaced."

"Just temporarily while you're on leave." The guy at his desk stood and walked over to him before she could say anything. "I'm Adams." He jerked his head toward the other one and held out his hand. "That's Murphy. He's the permanent replacement for Jackson."

"He's got big shoes to fill," Greg said as he shook Adams' hand. There was something that didn't feel quite right in the handshake. It wasn't as strong as he was used to with the other cops in the office. "They don't come much better than Jackson." He wasn't sure how he felt about Jackson being replaced so quickly. The captain hadn't said anything about replacements, but it was bound to happen sooner or later; he just figured it'd be one of the guys from the precinct, someone he already knew. Getting used to a stranger in Jackson's seat was going to be a lot harder.

"I heard he was a great cop. It's such a loss." Adams pursed his lips and frowned. "And only two months to go before he retired. What a shame." His words sounded rehearsed and insincere.

Casey walked around the room sniffing at everyone's feet and legs. Several of the officers reached down and petted him. When he got to Carter, he sniffed his shoes and growled.

"Casey, what's wrong?" Greg shook his head and stared at Casey. His gut knotted, wondering what his dog was trying to tell him, and worried that it wasn't good. "Sorry, Carter. I've never known him to growl like that at anyone, and he's met you before. You must have something on your shoes he doesn't like the smell of."

Carter shrugged. "You may be right. It might be the new cream I put on my athlete's foot."

"Could be. He doesn't like medicinal smells. Anyway—" Greg outwardly brushed off his concerns, gesturing like it was nothing "—captain said to find a beach with hot men somewhere for a couple of months, and I'm taking him up on it. We're leaving this afternoon. Hawaii, here I come."

The officers gathered around. Some patted his back while others shook his hand. It felt like he was leaving his close family, but Greg couldn't shake the feeling that one of them had betrayed him and Jackson. One or more of them was working with the Black Fins and he couldn't let himself relax until he knew who.

As Greg got ready to leave, Carter knelt down by Casey. He reached into his pocket and pulled out a dog treat. "Here, Casey. Let's be friends. My Buck likes these things."

Casey again growled and slunk on his stomach toward Greg, leaving the biscuit on the floor. Greg wondered what Casey knew that he couldn't tell anyone. His grandfather had always said to trust a dog's instincts. Greg tried to remember if Casey had ever shown any issues with Carter before.

Adams reached down and petted Casey. "Nice dog you have there. Wouldn't want to leave him here, would you?" He ruffled Casey's neck.

"No way." Greg grinned. "We've been apart too much while I was in rehab." Casey was too important for him to leave behind. He was the only real family Greg had left in the world.

* * *

Out in the car, Greg took a moment and rubbed Casey over. A sharp prick caught his finger as he passed it near Casey's collar. "What have you got here, boy?" Greg removed the collar. A tiny, high-tech radio-tracking device was attached. He'd caught his finger on the minute antenna.

"Somebody's trying to follow us." Greg pulled it off the collar and set it on his dash. The thing was too small to do anything more than transmit his location. With all the squad room petting Casey, anyone could've slipped the thing on him.

Greg started the car and headed back to his hotel. "If someone's going to this much trouble to keep track of me, Jackson and I must've been really close to uncovering something before that raid went south. Maybe I've been looking at this the wrong way, Casey. I need to look at what I know. What Jackson knew. Or try and figure out what someone thinks we knew. This is a lot more than just a simple case of them putting a hit out on me."

He turned down the road to his motel. "We need to get this worked out quickly. I just hope we're doing the right thing by leaving town."

Casey cocked his head and whined as if that was the answer Greg was missing.

He rubbed Casey's head as he turned into the parking lot. "Yeah, you're right. Let's put some distance on things and see what happens. Sometimes the chicken doesn't stick its head out of the coop if the fox is watching too closely."

* * *

Back at the motel room, Greg called the captain on the burner phone. "I found something on Casey's collar." He turned on the lamp and looked at the tiny thing in brighter light. It looked mass produced. He wondered if the manufacturer kept records of who bought their equipment, but it was a little dinged up. It might've been bought second hand.

"What?"

He dropped the tracker on the desk and walked over to the window. He was suddenly worried someone might try and do something before he left town. "Looks like a small tracking device."

"Any idea who put it there?"

"It could have been anyone." There had been too many people in the squad room. Looking back, Greg wondered if there were even any beat cops out writing parking tickets. It was like everyone on the day shift had been there. "Several of the guys were petting him."

"He growled at Carter. Do you think it might have been him?"

Greg's gut tightened at the thought. He'd swear on a stack of Bibles Carter was a good cop. "I don't want to think so. He's been around Carter before and never reacted that way. Like Carter said, it could have been the smell of the ointment on his feet."

"Is that gadget big enough to get prints off of?"

Greg picked the transmitter up again. "Probably the only ones you'll get are mine. It really isn't any bigger than a dime."

"Okay." The captain paused. "Tell you what. Put it in your car. When Carter picks the car up, the tracker will go with it."

"I think I have a better idea." Greg snickered. "There's a car in the parking lot with a Florida license plate." He'd always prided himself on his powers of observation, it was just one of the things that made him a good detective. He just hoped no one got hurt from his plan. He might never forgive himself if some innocent traveler ended up hurt because he was trying to throw a bad guy off the trail. He also hoped the car was heading back to Florida, and not staying in town for any

42

extended reason. Greg was fairly sure it had just appeared in the parking lot the previous evening.

Wood cackled. "I like the way you think. That's what makes you a good cop. Watch your back."

Greg chuckled. "Don't worry. I intend to."

Even with Casey along, he stayed extra vigilant as he placed the tracker on the car, after recording its information so he could try and contact the manufacturer and maybe get a lead that way. Every time Casey paused, Greg looked around, half expecting someone to ambush them from behind the dumpster.

* * *

An hour later, Carter showed up at the motel. He had a pet carrier just like Casey's and a Sheltie that, from a distance, looked like Casey's twin. "I think we're good to go. I'm on a flight that leaves here in two hours."

They exchanged keys.

Casey walked up to Carter with his tail wagging and sniffed at the other dog.

"Oh, by the way, captain wants us to also trade dog carriers."

"Why?" Greg didn't want to sound too suspicious, but since Casey wasn't a big fan of Carter all of a sudden, he was on watch for any little change in the plan. He really hoped Carter wasn't one of the bad cops. Although Casey seemed less antagonistic toward Carter since they were out of the squad room.

Carter shrugged and opened his dog carrier. "He didn't say, and I didn't ask."

Greg grinned. "Best do what he says." It didn't take them long to get the fake Casey into Casey's carrier.

Carter left driving Greg's new Impala.

Greg packed his and Casey's gear into the Ford Explorer, including a canvas shopping bag filled with his grandmother's quilt, and hit the road.

Two blocks from the motel, Greg pulled into the parking lot of a large grocery store. He took time to drop the dog crate in the big dumpster behind the building. It was a little more dinged up than he liked and he didn't want to risk there being something hidden in it that could prove problematic to either him or Casey. He also went over the Explorer as best he could with the limited tools he had. He didn't find any tracking devices, but the thing was LoJacked. They'd be able to track that if they knew the codes. He suddenly wished he was riding a horse into the mountains. It'd be harder to track. He then headed to the local hardware store to pick up a few tools. If he was going to be stuck in the mountains all winter, he wanted something to do in case the internet went down—he could only read so many books. Since all his wood carving tools had been in the garage when the house burned, he had to buy all new ones. With the captain footing part of the bill, he went with the really nice ones, and picked up a good supply of wood to keep him occupied. He just hoped he bought enough sandpaper to last through the deepest snow. A supply of paints and brushes filled out his purchase.

Chapter Seven

GREG PULLED into the parking lot of a grocery store in
Government Camp. He rubbed Casey's head. "I know the captain said
his cousin was going to stock the cabin, Casey, but you know I'm
picky about some things. I also know you like a certain brand of treats.
Stay here, I'll be right back. It's cool enough; you'll be okay." He got
out of the car and took a deep breath of the cool mountain air that
carried a hint of snow. The snowy peak of Mt. Hood stood high and
mighty to the northeast.

Fifteen minutes later, he returned with a couple of bags and two
cases of Coke which he placed in the back of the Explorer. "I think
we're all set, Casey. Rotisserie chicken for tonight and sandwich
makings for tomorrow. We'll have to see what Bob left in the cabin
before we do any more shopping."

Casey wagged his tail, whined, and tried to get over the back of
the seat.

Greg pulled on his collar. "Oh, no you don't. No chicken until
supper."

The dog obediently sat back in the front seat.

Greg rubbed Casey's ears, started the engine, and backed out of
the parking space. Just getting out of the city was enough to help him
relax more than he'd done in months. But he warned himself to not
forget to watch out. There was still the possibility of danger. If anyone

had the captain's office bugged they might be waiting for him at the cabin and no one would find his body for months.

* * *

"Damn!" Greg gripped the steering wheel tight as he hit another rut. Pain shot up his leg as he applied the clutch and brought the Explorer to a stop. Even though the gunshot wound was mostly healed, quick, jerky movements still caused his strained knee to hurt.

Since he'd left Trillium Lake Road, the tall trees on each side of the narrow track left barely enough room for a vehicle to pass. Their thick branches allowed only small bits of sunlight to reach the ground.

"Casey, I must be out of my mind. Why did I allow the captain to talk me into this? Being out here isn't going to help me find the Black Fins. This is stupid. I hope that cabin is close. I'd hate for us to have to sleep in the car. There isn't room to turn around, and I have no desire to back this thing all the way to the highway in the dark." It was late enough, if he had to go back to the highway, it was going to be long past sundown when he reached pavement. He knew he was being bitchy, but he was tired and hungry, and his leg hurt. The city seemed so far away. How was he ever going to survive out in the wilderness?

He rubbed his leg to ease the pain, put the car back in gear, and moved forward.

Suddenly, the track widened into a clearing. Greg applied the brakes and the Explorer slid to a stop on pine needles. He gasped at his first sight of the lake. The trees across the water hid the setting sun, but its rays painted the clouds above with vibrant reds, oranges, and yellows and made the lake look like it was on fire. To his right sat an A-frame cabin. The front of the cabin was all glass that also reflected the colors of the sky. The roof was covered with solar panels, and a satellite dish attached to one wall pointed toward a nearby peak. A covered porch spanned the width of the front. Two rockers sat to one side of the door with a table between them. The sight lightened Greg's spirits. "Maybe this won't be so bad after all, Casey. Looks like we've got all the conveniences of home. I wonder if the water's hot. I sure could use a hot bath for my knee after this drive." He rubbed Casey's ears. "Yeah, I know. You don't want a bath, but I bet you'd like to stretch your legs." He opened the car door and the dog jumped down and headed for the closest tree. "Stay close, buddy. Don't need you getting lost, and I'd hate to have to come looking for you; it's going to be dark soon."

He opened the back door of the Explorer and removed a small suitcase and the bags from the store, carried them to the cabin, set them on the porch, and then went back for one of the cases of Coke and the bag with the quilt. "Come on, Casey. Let's get inside. We'll unpack everything else in the morning."

Unlocking the door, he went into the cabin and looked around. Casey bounded ahead of him ready to sniff everything in the place. The light from the setting sun illuminated the main room. Its colors enhanced those of the décor. Log walls were hung with colorful rugs and afghans in orange, yellow, mauve, and tan. A large sofa in dark brown was covered with throw pillows of the same colors.

He went back out and carried in the suitcase, bags, and Coke. Setting the suitcase on a chair and the bags and Coke on a bar between the living area and kitchen, he flipped a light switch. An overhead fixture burst into light. There was a note on the kitchen counter.

Welcome, Greg. Hope you find everything okay. Don said you might have trouble navigating the stairs to the loft so I left all of the clothes in the suitcases in the living room. The sofa opens out into a queen-sized bed. Feel free to help yourself to anything here. Clean sheets and towels are in the closet next to the bathroom.

Under the note was a stack of instruction manuals for the kitchen appliances, the generator, and other mechanical items. "Looks like I have some reading to do, Case."

A quick turn of the kitchen sink faucet brought clear water that soon ran hot. "Looks like I'm in luck for hot water, Casey. Now let's see if this place has a bathroom."

A door beside the kitchen led to a small bathroom. "Darn! Looks like I'll have to make do with a shower. I'm glad I packed the heating pad in the overnight case. I almost put it into the big suitcase."

Stepping out of the bathroom, he looked at the stairs leading to the loft bedroom. "Captain was right about the stairs, Casey. I think you and I'll be sleeping on the pull-out sofa. At least until the knee feels better."

The suitcase Bob left contained five pairs of jeans, several t-shirts, a couple of plaid flannel shirts, sweat shirts and pants, underwear, and socks. A heavy canvas coat was draped over the back of the chair. "Well, Casey, looks like I'll be dressed and warm for a few days anyway." He placed the suitcase on a chair next to his. "No closet down here."

A coat rack hung on the wall next to the front door, and he hung the coat on one of the pegs.

Greg emptied the bags of groceries he'd gotten in Government Camp, and whipped up a pot of coffee. A quick check of the fridge revealed it was full of his favorite beer, Coke, and fresh vegetables. The freezer was well stocked with hamburger patties and chicken breasts in individual plastic bags along with a couple of bags of frozen fries and some vegetables. Next to the fridge was a small pantry with cans of vegetables, beans, fruits, and several varieties of soup in addition to cans of Casey's favorite dog food and a box of treats. "Looks like Bob thought of just about everything, Casey."

A trip outside with Casey revealed a significant drop in the temperature since the sun set. Stars filled the night sky. It was more brilliant than any view he'd personally seen before and for a moment Greg wished he had something more than his flip phone camera to capture the scene. He crossed his arms and shivered slightly as he looked up at the Milky Way where it cut a swatch across the sky. Looking up at the vastness made him feel small and insignificant. But he didn't dwell on those feelings. He needed to get focused on finding the Black Fins.

Greg sat on one of the rockers and rubbed his arms. If this was an indication of the weather in the coming few months, he was going to need those sweatshirts. He rose and walked around the cabin. A large pile of wood stood outside the back door. He picked up an armload, whistled for Casey, and went back inside. It didn't take him long to remember his Boy Scout training and get a fire going. The gentle crackling made it easy for him to relax. He'd never really been a country boy, but being away from the city was easier than he'd expected it to be. There was a lot of opportunity to finish healing in the quiet cabin, but he wanted to find the men who'd killed Jackson.

After he put his grandmother's quilt on the back of the couch, Greg booted up the laptop, quickly realizing the internet connection was slower than he was used to, but he didn't mind. He sent the captain an email to let him know he'd arrived okay. He also mentioned the strange switch of carriers and ask the captain to see about restricting access to the LoJack information on the Explorer. If Carter was part of the problem, it might already be too late for that, but he had to try. He was thankful his police logins still worked. The captain had left him active. He continued digging into the members of the police force, hoping something would jump out at him. There had to be an answer somewhere, and even if it had been staring him in the face, Greg hoped his change of scenery might help spur his mind enough to put the pieces together.

He took a break and baked a potato and warmed the chicken in the microwave. After feeding Casey, he sat on the couch with his grandmother's quilt around his shoulders. The quilt gave him a feeling of comfort. It was as if she had her arms wrapped around him.

Casey jumped up beside him and he brushed him while they watched a cop drama on TV. "Boy, I don't know if I'm going to like the trees around here or not. You seem to have picked up a bunch of needles."

When the show was over, he watched the news for any hint the Black Fins had been active, let Casey out for a few minutes, and then went back to the computer.

Chapter Eight

GREG WALKED out onto the porch with his coffee, the next morning. He'd slept longer than he planned, but he'd been up until the wee hours researching things. The quiet had made it hard for him to go to sleep. He'd never stopped to realize how much he relied on the background sounds of the city to lull him to sleep each night. But once he'd fallen asleep, he'd had one of the best sleeps in years. He woke wondering if the thinner air was responsible for it. The damp, chilly air made him glad of the heavy sweaters Bob left him.

Casey ran down the steps and around the yard stopping every three or four feet to hike his leg on another bush or tree. He seemed very happy to spend time claiming the yard as his. For him, the Black Fins didn't exist. He was just thrilled he and Greg were getting to spend some time out, alone in the wilderness.

Greg grinned. He was happy to know he and Casey were alive and back together. The start of the morning made him wish he could just walk away from the department and retire to the woods. Maybe he could take up writing crime novels, or sell little carved critters at the store down the mountain. "Marking your territory, Casey? Better watch out. There's apt to be something bigger than you in those woods that doesn't like having you around, and don't pick up any more fir needles than you have to." He sat on one of the rocking chairs and leaned back. "This is nice. Don't know what will happen when winter sets in, but right now, I like it."

A large shadow momentarily flashed across the lush grass of the clearing and drew Greg's attention upwards. There was nothing visible, no cloud, not even a bird. He wondered what could cause it. Maybe a super-sonic plane, but where was the sound? His gut suddenly tightened, worried it might be a drone or something trying to keep track of him. "Come on, Casey. We need to get the car unloaded. With this knee, it's going to take a while." He gulped down the last of his coffee and set the cup on the porch rail as the shadow passed again, this time from the other direction. It was too fast for him to see what was making it, although it looked like a huge bird of some kind. Greg suddenly felt trapped among all the trees that limited his view. Sure, he could see the lake, but other than that and the vista beyond it, he was cut off. There was little he could see around him, other than directly above or out to the north. The safety and security of the place suddenly felt like the exact opposite. At least in the city, things were more open and exposed. The trees suddenly closed in on him and he didn't like it. There was too much he didn't know out in the wilds.

* * *

Making his morning commute from his cave on Mt. Hood to the small cabin by the lake, Kynth looked down at the neighboring cabin. It was strange to see an unfamiliar car in front of Bob's cabin. Bob hadn't said anything about coming out this late in the year, and he'd never known him to let anyone else use the place. He banked around and flew back over the area. This time, a small dog followed a man carrying a box from the car to the building. Bob was allergic to dogs. Kynth decided he'd better check things out. He folded his wings and swooped downward. As he neared the ground, he twisted so he landed on his hind feet. When his feet touched the ground, they were already human and encased in hiking boots.

* * *

51

Greg limped toward the cabin carrying a box of books. His knee complained about bearing the weight without the help of his cane. He suddenly wished he'd switched to e-books and didn't have to lug so much weight around.

Casey growled from the porch. He glared behind Greg with his tail low and out and his ears flattened to his head.

A deep voice from behind Greg said, "Looks like you could use some help."

Greg dropped the box and spun around. The action caused a twinge to his knee. He wished he'd put his gun on, but it was so quiet here he'd left it inside. "Quiet, Casey."

"Careful," the man said as Greg stumbled a couple of steps, fighting to remain standing.

A soft low laugh caused a tingle down Greg's spine. In his agitated state, he wasn't sure if the voice was sexy or dangerous.

The man seemed oblivious to Greg's nervousness as he strolled toward him. "Hope there's nothing breakable in that box." His voice had a lilting quality and a faint accent Greg couldn't place.

Greg leaned over, rubbed his knee, and looked at the vision before him. The man was well over Greg's six feet tall with almost white hair. It wasn't gray, but a light platinum blond. His faded jeans fit like a second skin, and his tight green t-shirt clung to a perfect six-pack of abs. Green eyes that matched his shirt twinkled as he smiled. He looked more like a model than someone who'd be out hiking around an Oregon mountain lake. Under other circumstances, Greg would've been instantly attracted, but he was on edge and his adrenaline made him want to protect himself and Casey from the stranger. He wondered if the man was a neighbor. The captain had mentioned another cabin close by. He hadn't heard any vehicles coming close. Then he remembered the shadow. If it had been a drone, the man might be investigating what it saw. As he straightened up, Greg really wished his pistol wasn't lying near the couch in the cabin.

Casey growled again and jumped from the porch to stand between the man and Greg.

"Sorry to startle you. You can call off the dog. I'm friendly." The man held up both hands, palms toward Greg. "I saw lights here last night and thought maybe Bob came down for a few days before bad weather sets in."

Keeping his eyes on the stranger, Greg leaned over and put a hand on Casey's head. "It's okay, buddy." He hoped he wasn't opening them both up to more danger. With any luck, they could get the books into the cabin, and he could grab his pistol and slip it inside his waistband without the stranger noticing.

The man stepped closer and held out a large hand. "I'm Ken. I have a cabin across the cove."

"Greg." He wondered if this guy was legit or not. Was he really a friend of Bob, or had the bad guys in the department followed him? He'd better be careful. As they shook hands, heat encased his. The man's hand must be several degrees warmer than his. "Aren't you cold in just a t-shirt?"

"I seldom feel cold. I have a higher than normal body temperature, and it keeps me warm from inside." Ken turned and pulled another box out of the Explorer. "I've never known Bob to let anyone stay here. Especially with a dog since he's allergic to them."

"I work for Bob's cousin. The doctor recommended a place to rest and recuperate; Bob told my boss I could stay here." Greg picked up the dropped box, walked up the steps to the porch, and through the open door into the cabin. "The boss didn't say anything about an allergy. He knew I was bringing Casey."

"With that leg, are you sure you should be out in the wild?" Ken followed him into the cabin. "This late in the season, you never know when we might get snowed in."

Greg set the box on the floor next to the couch. He rubbed his knee with one hand and slipped his pistol in the back of his jeans with the other as he turned to face Ken. "The knee isn't as bad as it looks. It's getting better every day, and I think I have sufficient supplies to last until spring if I'm frugal. Do you live out here year round?"

"Yeah. I like the solitude." Ken set his box next to Greg's. "I'm a writer."

"You probably get asked this a lot." Greg grinned, he'd been thinking about doing that in the quiet. "What do you write?"

Ken ran his fingers through that thick, silvery hair. "I write gay fiction with a little fantasy and paranormal thrown in."

Greg's heart beat a little faster at the thought of replacing Ken's fingers with his own. He chuckled and winked. "You probably get asked this a lot also, but anything I might have read?"

Ken grinned and told him a couple of titles.

Greg's mouth dropped open. They were books that had graced his shelves in the house. He hadn't had time to replace them since the fire. There'd been a lot on his mind since then. The books he had with him were ones the captain lent him to get through the winter, mostly mysteries and crime novels. "I loved that series about the shape shifters. I've often thought how amazing it would be if such creatures actually existed."

Ken quirked an eyebrow. "Who says they don't?"

Greg shrugged. "Well, I've never seen one. Have you?"

"I've seen a lot of amazing things in my lifetime." He leaned against the chair where Greg's suitcase was. He looked incredibly relaxed and overly sexy. "You'll have to ask Bob. Besides, I've never seen the wind. Have you?"

"No. Just the motion of the trees caused by it." Greg turned toward the kitchen. "Hey, I could use another cup of coffee. How about you?"

Ken pointed his thumb toward the door. "Why don't I bring in that last box while you get it?"

"Fine." Greg didn't want to let on how much he liked the idea of not having to do a final trip between the truck and the cabin. "Let's have it on the porch. How do you drink it?"

"Just coffee for me."

"I like sugar in mine. My grandmother always said I don't drink coffee, I drink sugar dissolved in brown water."

The Black Fin Case

As Ken went out the door chuckling, Greg watched and admired the fit of his jeans. Surely, with the stuff he writes, he must be gay. He thought a fling might be what he needed to get his mind off of the guys who were trying to kill him. But he wasn't sure he wanted to put anyone in the line of fire if the bad guys tracked him down.

Ken set the last box on the porch as Greg came out with the coffee and a dog biscuit.

Casey sat at the bottom of a tree barking at a chittering squirrel. With a sharp yip, Casey ran to the other side of the tree. He seemed to have already forgotten about growling at Ken.

Placing the cups on a table between the two rockers, Greg called, "Come, Casey. Leave the wild animals alone. You wouldn't know what to do with that squirrel if you caught him." He'd often been thankful Casey wasn't quick enough to catch either the squirrels or rabbits he'd always barked at in the back yard of the house. He wasn't sure *he'd* know what to do with them either, other than throw the carcasses away.

Ken sat on one of the rockers and picked up a cup. "So tell me, how'd you hurt the knee?" He sipped from the cup.

"I got shot." After handing Casey the biscuit, Greg sat in the other chair and reached for his cup.

Casey dropped at his feet and chewed the biscuit.

Ken jerked in surprise. "Shot as in 'bang, bang shoot 'em up'?" He held up his thumb and forefinger in a shooting motion.

Greg snorted and assumed the position of holding a machine gun. "More like 'rat-ta-ta-ta-ta-tat."

"Whoa!" Ken's jaw dropped. "What happened?"

"I'm a policeman. We were on a drug raid. They knew we were coming and ambushed us. My partner was killed, and I took a bullet to the leg." He took a drink. There was an odd feeling and he wondered why he was opening up to the stranger. It was like some force of some kind was compelling him. If Ken wasn't what he said. If he was someone the bad cops sent to do him in, it wouldn't matter. He hoped Ken was just an author and maybe they could be friends. It would help the winter pass easier. "A day or two before I was supposed to get out of rehab, a guy came into the place and tried to kill me. An orderly and I chased him off. Then the night after I got out of rehab, someone firebombed my house." Reaching down, he rubbed behind Casey's ears. "It's thanks to Casey I got out. His barking woke me, and we went out the window. The guy was waiting and started shooting at us. Casey was grazed by a bullet, and I landed on the bad leg and twisted my knee." He sighed and took another sip. Talking about the fire was getting easier. He wasn't sure if that was a good thing or not. "Luckily, I didn't need more surgery. Just have to wear this brace for a couple of months. With all that, the captain put me on vacation and sent me up here."

"That sucks." Ken finished his coffee.

"I lost everything in the house." Greg winked. "Even several of your books. The only things I rescued were Casey and a quilt my grandmother made."

"We'll have to see about replacing the books." Ken grinned. "Maybe even signed copies this time." He changed the subject. "We're apt to get some bad weather soon. You should be okay with the solar power unless we have a long period of no sunshine and your batteries run out of stored power. Do you know how to operate a generator?"

Greg sighed. He was a detective, not a mechanic. What he knew about small engines and generators could probably fill a corner of a napkin. "Captain said there's one in the shed. I'm hoping I don't have to use it. Bob left an instruction manual, but I haven't really looked at it yet."

Ken stood. "I'll come back in a day or two and go over it with you. If you need anything before then, see that flag on the corner of the porch?" He gestured toward the corner of the porch closest to the lake.

Greg followed where he pointed. A red cloth hung there, attached to a metal pole. "Yeah."

"Just run it up the pole, and I'll see it and check on you."

"Just where is your cabin?"

Ken pointed across the small cove. "Just on the other side of those trees. You can't see the cabin, but you may see my smoke sometimes. I can see the flag from my porch. Anyway, nice to meet you, but I'd better get going. My muse is calling."

"Muse?" It wasn't a term Greg was used to and Ken's phone hadn't rung, if he even had a cell phone on him. He hadn't seen any indication of one in Ken's tight jeans.

"Yeah. The thing in my head that tells me what and when to write. You may have just given me a new plot. Something about a cop who gets shot." He reached down and patted Casey's head. "See you later, Casey. Take care of your master."

Casey sniffed of the hand and then licked it. It almost surprised Greg there was no growling this time. He trusted Casey's judgement of character and wondered if the initial reaction had been the strangeness of the surrounding and Ken just appearing like he had.

"Good. We're friends now." Ken stepped off of the porch and left.

Greg watched him walk into the woods, and then turned and went inside. There were a couple of things he wanted answered. He took the burner cellphone out of his pocket. He was a little surprised to see he actually had a signal. It was only two bars, but it would be enough. He dialed the captain.

"Wood."

"Hey, Captain." He glanced out the window, toward the trees where Ken had disappeared. "I need for you to check someone out for me."

"Who?"

"His name's Ken. He didn't give a last name, but he's a writer, and if he's who he says he is, I've read some of his work, and he looks like the picture on the back. Last name there is Draig. Says he's a friend of Bob's. Seems okay, but I want to be sure." Even if Jackson hadn't died in an ambush, and his house hadn't been firebombed, Greg would've checked Ken out. He'd been a cop long enough to be suspicious of everyone he encountered.

"Okay. I'll check with Bob and let you know. How's everything else?"

"Cabin's good. I didn't try the stairs to the loft; I thought I'd wait until the knee's better. Don't want to fall out here in the middle of nowhere with no one but Casey around." He touched on little things he hadn't mentioned in the email he sent first thing.

"Sounds like a good idea to me." The captain snorted. "Don't know if we could get an ambulance out that far."

"Right. Bob did a good job of stocking stuff. I stopped in Government Camp and picked up a few things. This Ken guy says unless we get a lot of days without sunshine, I should be okay for power. He offered to show me how the generator works. I think I'm good until spring, or you catch the bad guys, whichever happens first. I'm counting on you catching the bad guys." He didn't bother adding he hadn't found much in his digging. Everyone was just too clean. It didn't feel right. There had to be something he could use.

"I'll bet Casey likes it."

Greg chuckled. "He's not sure how to react. I think he's marked everything in the yard. I don't know if he's annoying the squirrels or if they're annoying him. Just hope he doesn't run into anything bigger."

Captain Wood laughed. "Well, the bears should be in hibernation soon if not already. I'll get back with you as soon as I find out anything about this Ken."

When he got off the call, Greg continued to stare into the woods. Ken had disappeared so quickly, but the trees were so thick anyone could get within a hundred yards of the cabin before he spotted them, maybe closer. Greg suppressed a shudder. He went in, poured another cup of coffee, and settled on a stool at the bar to clean his pistol. There was only so much he could do to be ready if the bad guys showed up, but he wanted to do what he could.

* * *

As soon as Ken was far enough away from the cabin to not be seen, he resumed his natural shape. He thought back over the events of the morning and decided it might be an interesting winter. He'd felt an immediate attraction to Greg. After all, it had been a long time since he'd taken a lover. Not that there was a large selection of gay men on the mountain. He was sure a little interaction between him and Greg might prove interesting; it would definitely break up the long lonely winter.

* * *

Greg was watching a movie, eating a sandwich, and drinking a Coke when his cellphone rang a couple of hours later. The captain's burner number was on the screen.

Greg swallowed a bite of sandwich and answered in a low voice, "Yo."

"Do you always answer the phone like that?" the captain asked.

"No, you know that. But I didn't want my voice recognized if it wasn't you calling. Did you find out anything?" He washed down the sandwich with a gulp of Coke.

"Oh, yeah. Bob thought it was funny I was checking on Ken."

"So, what did he say?" At least this information was something he was able to get quickly.

"First that he's okay. You're not in any danger from him except for the fact he's gay."

Greg grinned to himself. "I already picked up on that." Having concrete confirmation made Greg wonder if Ken would be interested in them warming up the winter a little bit.

"He said you can trust him with your life."

"I guess I kind of am." But having someone he trusted vouch for Ken made it easier to think about their next meeting.

"Ken was there when Bob built the cabin twenty years ago and doesn't look a day older than when they first met. Said he's older than he looks. He also said to be prepared for anything, and to only believe half of what you see."

"Wonder what he meant by that." Greg frowned and scratched his chin. He hadn't shaved that morning, and his chin was rough with stubble. That sounded almost ominous, and he wasn't sure what to make of it. It sounded like that old adage his grandmother used to tell him, *Believe nothing that you hear and only half of what you see.*

Captain Wood gave a half laugh. "Didn't say. Just said to tell you some things aren't always what they seem. How'd you meet the guy anyway?"

"He just showed up this morning while I was unloading the car." Again Greg wondered about the guy just appearing out of the trees, then vanishing so quickly. But if he'd been in the area for over twenty years, he probably knew all the trails, even ones that weren't overly obvious to a city boy like himself. If Ken was older than he looked, that made Greg curious too. He didn't mind older guys, he actually preferred them to younger men. They tended to be more stable. He'd gotten tired of flighty guys back in college.

"Keep on your toes."

"Will do. Roger and out." Even though the captain couldn't see him, Greg gave a quick salute and grinned.

"Smart ass." Laughter boomed over the phone. "I know you just saluted."

Greg didn't bother replying. He simply ended the call and pulled his computer from the coffee table into his lap. He wanted to see if he could figure out a bit more about Ken. He pulled up one of Ken's books on Amazon and clicked on the author's bio.

Ken Draig is a semi recluse living in the wilds of Oregon. He rarely makes public appearances, but spends his time pumping out bestselling stories of fantasy one after the other. His research into the Middle Ages makes his readers feel as if they were really there.

A Google search didn't return much more information. There was no date or place of birth.

Chapter Nine

KEN WALKED into the clearing a couple of days later and found Greg splitting firewood with Casey lying nearby. He'd cloaked himself in invisibility, so he stood there watching for a couple of minutes.

Casey looked in his direction, cocked his head sideways, and sniffed the air. He gave a short huff, then laid his head on his paws as if to say he didn't find anything threatening in Ken's scent.

Ken admired the play of Greg's muscles under the tight sweat-dampened long-sleeved knit shirt he wore. Dropping the invisibility while behind Greg, he said, "That looks like fun – not."

Greg spun around, ax raised as if ready to attack. He grinned and lowered the tool. "One of these times, you're going to sneak up on me when I have my gun. I'd hate to shoot you."

"Oh, I wouldn't worry about it." Ken smiled back. He didn't know Greg well enough to explain how bullets wouldn't do much more than irritate him unless a bullet hit a vital organ. "Why are you splitting wood? It can't be good on your knee."

"Bob left a whole list of things to do. One was to keep the wood box full in case of snow."

Bob was a fairly sensible guy, and always kept a good supply of wood and other things he needed for life at the lake. Ken was thankful he didn't need as much as the humans did. "What else?"

"Be sure the oil lamps are full. They'll help preserve the energy in the solar batteries. Clean the chimney on a regular basis." He gave a soft laugh. "Not sure I understand that one. Also, he said to know where the matches are. What's up?"

Ken wasn't sure Greg would be able to get up on the roof to clean the chimney with his bum knee. It wouldn't be a big problem for him to do it for Greg. "Taking a walk to clear my head and thought I'd go over that generator with you. As to the chimney, he could have meant two things. The chimneys on the lamps can get smoky on the inside, and fir needles can cause a fire in the chimney on the cabin. He has a screen over the top of it, so it should be okay until the soot builds up. Hopefully you'll be up getting on the roof by then, or I can handle it for you."

Greg buried the blade of the ax in the stump he was using as a chopping block, picked up the jacket lying on one of the un-split rounds and put it on. "I think the generator's in the shed."

"Why the jacket now?" Ken was a little sorry to see Greg's muscles muted by the heavy fabric. He always forgot how delicate humans could be in the weather. It always seemed like they were either putting clothes on or taking them off. He'd rather Greg take more off than put them on.

"I'm sweaty. Don't want to get chilled." Greg looked at Ken and shook his head. "I don't know why you aren't cold in just a shirt."

"Like I said, I have a high body temperature. Also I've been up here for years. You get to the point the cold doesn't affect you as much."

"Don't know about that. I doubt I'll ever be able to run around in just a t-shirt if it's below 45 degrees."

Inside the shed, Ken showed Greg how to fire up the generator. He'd learned a few years earlier when Bob had been there in the winter and fallen off the roof cleaning the chimney. Ken had to set Bob's broken leg since Bob hadn't wanted him to fly him down the mountain to the hospital. That was probably for the best. Flying down would've potentially exposed him, even if the technology fifteen years ago was less than what he was used to in the modern world. It would have to be an extremely special case to make him go flying anywhere near town with the way the humans had everything wired, either radar, video, or camera phones. Flying over Government Camp was risky enough, even invisibly. The closest airport was several miles away and he could stay under the radar, but he still had to be careful. "You need to be sure there's plenty of propane." He wiped the dust off the gauge on the tank so he could read it. "Looks like it's full so you shouldn't have any problems." He proceeded to spend a few minutes showing Ken how to set the thing to start and then what to have it set on to keep it going.

"Great. Problems I can do without."

Ken walked to the door and picked up the end of a coil of rope about one inch in diameter. "See this heavy rope?"

"Yeah."

"Watch." He tied one end to a post inside the shed, ran the other through a hole beside the door and pointed to the back porch. "Bob runs this to the back door. If you have to come out here in a storm, hold on to the rope and you won't lose your way. The snow can sometimes be blinding and you get disoriented." As they exited the door, Ken brushed his shoulder against Greg's.

Greg looked at him with questioning eyes.

Ken smiled, leaned in, and lightly brushed his lips against Greg's. He didn't normally ask permission on things or people he wanted. He just took them. He'd been able to feel Greg's attraction and wanted to see what his reaction would be. There wasn't any resistance. Ken's pulse picked up and he wondered how quickly he'd be able to move things along. It had been a long time since he'd been with someone, either one of his own kind, or a human.

Blushing slightly, Greg turned and closed the shed door, and they walked to the back door of the cabin, Ken holding the end of the rope. "I, ah, made some of those canned cinnamon rolls this morning. How about some coffee and a roll?"

"Sounds good." Ken secured the end of the rope to the rail of the back porch. He thought a roll with Greg might be just what he needed to get over his writer's block. After all, it had been nearly fifty years since he'd had more than a one-night-stand, and Greg was nice looking. They could have a very interesting winter. Greg hadn't jerked away at their impromptu kiss. He must be interested.

Inside the kitchen, Greg took off his gloves and jacket. "Have a seat in the living room; I'll bring the coffee and rolls."

Ken strolled into the living room. The sofa sleeper was open with the bed unmade. "I see you're sleeping on the couch?"

The microwave dinged.

"Yeah." Greg carried a tray with coffee and warm rolls and set it on the coffee table. The aroma of coffee rolled up around him. "I still haven't braved the stairs. If I fell, I could lie there all winter before someone came looking for me."

"Oh, I'd probably find you in a day or two. I told Bob the other night I'm keeping an eye on you." Ken sat on a chair, picked up a cup of coffee in one hand and a roll in the other. Even a few hours old, the roll still looked and smelled delicious. He couldn't resist and took a bite before he sipped his coffee.

Greg squinted as he sat on the unmade bed facing him. "Why? Do you think I need a babysitter?"

"No." Ken licked frosting from his lips seductively. The frosting was good, but he was in the mood to find out what Greg would taste like on his fingers. "But I know you're a city boy and not used to the mountains in winter. I'd do it for anyone, even if they weren't a good-looking cop."

Greg looked down at his coffee cup, and then raised his head and stared Ken in the eye. Beyond the rising color in his cheeks, there was an eagerness and look of loss and loneliness in that gaze. It called to Ken across the short distance separating them.

Ken stood, placed his cup on the table, took Greg's cup and placed it alongside his. He sat next to Greg, lifted his chin, and kissed him. "You know you're cute when you blush."

Greg returned the kiss and lay back on the bed pulling Ken down on top of him. By his eagerness, it was obvious it was going to be an interesting winter. Under Greg, a soft antique quilt cushioned them on the mattress that had seen better days. The combination of the bed with Greg was something Ken hadn't experienced before, but it felt good as he surrendered to Greg's lips and fingers.

Chapter Ten

THE CHILLY wind bit into Greg as he walked out onto the porch. The weather was rapidly changing from summer to winter. In the ten days he'd been at the cabin, the leaves were already changing. He'd never spent much time in the mountains, but it felt like there wasn't going to be much fall, not like closer to the coast. But then he could remember how early Mount Hood was dressed in a cloak of winter white, sometimes before Labor Day, and they were just past that.

Casey barked at something near the wood pile and a rabbit dashed for the porch with the dog in hot pursuit.

Greg laughed. At least Casey's chases were going better than his. He still had no clues as to the identity of the departmental leak. It was obvious he wasn't dealing with a stupid person. They were covering their tracks very well.

Movement near the edge of the trees caught his attention. Seconds later, Ken strolled into view, looking like he was out for a simple afternoon stroll. He had something over his right shoulder that Greg couldn't exactly make out. Greg glanced at the sun; it was still a few inches above the trees to the west. Ken must've gotten done with his writing early and came on over. They'd been spending every evening together since they started fooling around. He liked the way Ken felt in his arms. There was something very comfortable and easy about Ken. It had been years since Greg had found anyone he felt so whole with. Ken didn't seem to care he was a cop, or that a crazy gang was out to kill him. It was almost like Ken felt invulnerable to all of it.

As Ken drew closer, the item over his shoulder solidified into a fishing pole.

Casey stopped trying to get at the rabbit—which was probably long gone out the other side of the porch—and ran to greet Ken. The dog's complete acceptance of Ken also made it easy for Greg to relax around him and just enjoy their time together. Except for the first meeting, Casey hadn't growled at Ken once. They were best buds.

"Hey!" Greg walked to the edge of the porch. "What's with the fishing pole?"

"I figured we could catch us some dinner. I got my edits done and to my editor and didn't feel like diving into the new book." Ken walked up the steps and kissed Greg. "I just can't get the cop to come across as genuine as you do."

"Really?" Greg chuckled. Ken had told him about starting a new book that was more cop adventure than shifter romance. "Maybe I can read it sometime and give you some pointers. Cops aren't always easy to write about."

"Maybe you can." Ken linked his arm in Greg's and steered him down the steps and across the lawn. "But before you do that, we need to go catch some dinner. I'm hoping you know how to cook fish. I wouldn't want to invade your kitchen."

"Why not? You invade every other part of me." Greg enjoyed the way they could play with each other. Ken was a perfect blend of older man, and he still wasn't sure how much older, he was figuring forty or forty-five, max, even with his platinum blond hair. He was in too good a shape to be much older. Men tended to lose their muscle tone as they got older.

"Aye, I do love plundering your booty." Ken laughed. "You make me want to go back to being a pirate."

Greg pulled them to a stop and cocked an eye brow. "Being a pirate? Do tell."

Ken started them walking toward the dock again. "I should've said writing about a pirate. A lot of times when I really get into a story, I channel the characters. That's always a good sign it's going to be an awesome book. One of my early books, several years ago, was about a pirate and a silkie. It was a best seller."

"Yeah." Greg nodded. "I remember that one. *Holding His Skin.* The title was a little creepy, but it was a good book."

"Don't tell me about titles." He curled his lip. "I don't have the final say on them. The publishers do."

Greg looked at the dock as they approached. It was one of the parts of the property he hadn't explored. The boards were weathered and a little warped. He wasn't sure it would hold both their weights.

"It's safe," Ken said, as if reading his mind. "Bob comes out here all the time and he's heavier than you are. It might not look like it, but he does replace the boards when they reach the point they need it."

"Good." Greg still hesitated a bit as he put his foot on the first couple of boards. "It's getting cold enough, I'm not sure I want to go for a dip in the cold lake."

"If that happens, I promise to get you warm again." Ken didn't pause as he walked out to a couple of wooden chairs waiting for them at the dock's far end.

"You better." Greg followed him out and wasn't encouraged by Casey stopping to sniff the dock thoroughly before running back toward the wood pile presumably in search of another rabbit.

Ken pulled a small packet of something out of his pocket before loosening the line and freeing the hook. "If you want your own pole, I think Bob keeps a couple in the shed near the generator."

The Black Fin Case

Greg shook his head. He'd always found fishing rather boring, but was willing to endure a little bit of it to spend time with Ken. "No thanks. Not my thing. I'll just watch you."

"Okay." Ken flashed him a huge grin. "I like you watching me." He pulled something out of the pouch, put it on the hook, and then cast it out into the lake. With a contented sigh, he settled into the closest chair. "So how was your day? I'm hoping it was more interesting than mine. Edits can get old fast."

"So can looking for evidence that doesn't appear to exist." Greg eased himself into the other chair. There was a loud creak and he wasn't sure if it was from the chair or the dock. He really didn't want to fall into the lake.

"The trail is still cold." Ken cranked on his reel, then let off a bit. "I'd think in today's modern world, it would be really difficult to just make a paper trail disappear."

Greg shrugged and stared out across the lake. "Not all that hard if you've got the right people working for you. A good hacker can make a lot of things disappear if he wants to. I don't think a gang like the Black Fins would have someone like that on payroll, unless they're a lot more than just drug runners."

"More like what?" Ken cranked his line in, then cast it off again.

"That's what I can't figure out. Maybe they're an arm of the mafia. They might be part of the military." He sighed in frustration. In the past, he and Jackson had always talked things out and things would come to him. He'd spent several nights going over things with Ken and so far, nothing had popped into his head that sounded feasible. He was missing something, and it was huge. It was probably what the gang was trying to kill him for and he didn't even know what it was. It was possible the secret was something Jackson had learned and hadn't had time to tell him, but Jackson always told him everything important on a case as quickly as he learned it. It didn't make sense.

"Hey, give me a hand here." Ken interrupted Greg's thinking. "Got our first fish on the line." He cranked madly and soon a large trout appeared at the surface of the water and Ken quickly landed it.

Greg frowned at the fish. "Now what?"

Ken got the hook out of its mouth and handed the squirming thing to Greg. "I didn't bring a basket to put it in." He pulled out a small knife from his pocket, flipped it open and killed the fish. "Take it into the house. Put it in cold water in the sink. I'll clean them when I catch another one, then you can cook them."

The fish went limp in Greg's grasp, but still felt wet and slimy. "Okay. I hope you can tell me how you like it."

"Don't I always?" Ken laughed. "Trust me, it's going to be a great dinner."

Greg wasn't sure about that, but he hauled the fish into the kitchen and put it in cold water like Ken had instructed. Casey ran up to him, gave the fish a quick sniff and resumed his quest for rabbits. As he walked, Greg wondered what life would be like if he wasn't having to worry about the Black Fins finding him. He might get to like simple things like hanging out with Ken and fishing for their dinner. There was something basic and good about that.

* * *

Greg patted his stomach as he leaned his chair away from the table and looked at the remains of their dinner. He'd eaten a lot more than he'd planned, but the trout had been the best fish he'd ever eaten, let alone cooked. True to his word, Ken instructed him on what to do and it turned out great.

Ken pulled Greg close and kissed him. "You're a really good cook. You might end up putting a few pounds on me."

"Nah." Greg shook his head and stared at Ken. He couldn't imagine anything he did ever putting any extra weight on him. If he'd managed to keep his figure into his forties, he'd probably be in great shape the rest of his life, as long as nothing catastrophic happened. "You're going to look great forever."

"Thanks. You're pretty sexy yourself." He cupped Greg's face and kissed him again. "Okay. Let's get this cleaned up and settle in for a movie."

The Black Fin Case

Their last few movies had ended up with them just making out through most of the movie, even things they both loved. Greg was amazed how many of the same movies they both loved. He half expected Ken's taste to run toward romance or horror, based on what he wrote, but he liked science fiction, fantasy, comedy, and nearly anything gay. After the second night of going through the limited supply of movies Greg had brought, Ken showed up with the movie, more often than not.

"What do you want to watch tonight?" Greg picked up their plates and headed for the sink.

Ken followed him with the large serving platter with the remains of the fish. "It's been a while since I saw *Serenity*. The last time it was after spending all day on *Firefly*."

"Sounds good. I got the series watched a few weeks ago in rehab on my computer, but they turned out my lights before I could get to the movie." Greg put the dishes in the sink. Again it hit him how close to domestic bliss things with Ken were becoming. He hadn't been looking for it, but it felt nice and he was happier than he'd been in a very long time. If they could just put the Black Fins down, everything would be great. He might even welcome the idea of staying in the mountains with Ken for a while, or longer, if he wasn't having to look over his shoulder all the time for fear someone was about to put a bullet in his back.

Chapter Eleven

A POWDERING of snow covered the ground as Greg carried two cups of coffee out to where Ken sat watching Casey making his morning rounds. Casey handled the deep snow a lot better than Greg had been afraid he might.

Greg leaned over, kissed Ken's cheek, and handed him his cup. It hadn't been long, but greeting Ken every morning was becoming a comfortable routine. He'd never had a boyfriend for more than a couple of dates. The fact that Ken was still coming around after a couple of weeks made Greg feel good about things. Spending his nights with Ken and his days carving his little animals made his forced exile from the department almost enjoyable. Not that he didn't miss the city, but the captain was keeping him up-to-date on the progress of the case, and every day he checked for news on the computer. He'd all but given up on finding any leads on his own. The Black Fins were good at hiding their trails, better than any gang Greg had ever heard of. It was the only gloomy part of his time in the mountains. "Good morning, sunshine. Think it'll snow again today?"

Ken wrapped both of his hands around the hot cup and gave Greg a big smile. "Probably. It feels like it. Shouldn't last long though. It's early in the season, the storms are still building up their punch." He blew on his coffee and sipped it. "I'm going over to my cabin in a bit. Need to check on things and do a bit of writing."

Giving Ken his best cop stare, Greg put one hand on his hip and sipped his coffee. "I still don't understand why you can't write here."

Ken set his cup on the table. "Too many distractions." He pulled Greg down on his lap and nuzzled his neck. "See what I mean?"

"Careful. You'll make me spill my coffee." Greg turned, kissed him, and then snuggled on his shoulder. Ken had already figured out ways to distract him. He seemed to know instinctively the best way for any situation. "What did I do to deserve you?"

"Got shot." Ken chuckled softly.

Greg snorted and ran a hand through Ken's hair. "That I could have done without, but if it brought me you, it was worth it." He stood. "If you have to go, hurry back."

"I will." Ken finished his coffee and walked toward the woods.

Casey followed. He'd taken to doing that, and it was a good sign to Greg that Ken was a keeper. He just wasn't sure how everything with the Black Fins was going to play out and hated the idea Ken might get caught in the crossfire. The less he found on his searches, the more concerned he grew about the danger the gang posed to Greg and the people around him.

"Come back, Casey. You can't go with Ken this time."

The dog looked from Ken to Greg, and then trotted back to the porch. He lay down at Greg's feet, put his head on his paws and whined a bit as Ken disappeared into the trees.

* * *

Out of sight, Ken morphed into his natural form and took to the skies. As he flew toward Government Camp, a black SUV sped toward Lake Trillium. He circled the vehicle twice. It looked covert and government issue, maybe even black ops. The windows were all darker than regular tinting. Every dealer tag and emblem was missing. It was almost too sleek and shiny. Something in his gut told him to turn back. One advantage to living a long life, he'd learned centuries ago to listen to his gut. With frenzied wing beats, he made it back to the spot he'd taken off from in half the time it had taken him to get nearly to Government Camp. He landed quickly, shifted to his human form, and dashed toward Greg's cabin.

Greg was still on the porch, finishing his coffee. "You weren't gone long."

Ken frowned and tried to figure out the best way to explain things to Greg. "I think we have company."

"How do you know?" Greg gave Ken a dubious look, but he suddenly looked more apprehensive than Ken could remember seeing him since the first day when Ken had surprised him while he'd been carrying the box of books.

"Don't ask now; I'll explain later." He stepped up on the porch. He was used to people doing what he asked. Greg was a police officer. He was used to taking orders. Ken put a bit of command in his voice to get his attention. He didn't like the idea that he was bossing Greg around, but if it saved his life it would be worth it. "Greg, get your gun and don't be surprised by anything you see or hear. Don't let on like there's anything out of the ordinary." If he was going to pull off the plan that was slowly materializing, he was going to have a lot of explaining to do after everything was finished, but it didn't matter at that moment. The only thing that mattered was keeping Greg safe. He disappeared. "And don't talk to me. Just pretend I'm not here."

* * *

"What the . . .?" Greg's eyes opened wide and his jaw dropped. *This can't be happening. It's impossible.* Then he remembered what Bob had told the captain, *Things aren't always what they seem*, and *be prepared for anything*. But he wasn't sure *anything* included the man he'd been sleeping with just disappearing in front of him. Greg wasn't sure how he was supposed to react to that. People didn't just disappear. It wasn't possible.

Ken's voice sounded inside Greg's head. *"I said, don't react. If you want to say something to me, just think it."*

"Think it? Like telepathy in the movies, or in your books?" It sounded crazy. Greg felt crazy just accepting Ken's instructions, but

74

his gut told him to trust Ken. To that point, Ken had never done or said anything to give him pause.

"Exactly like that." Ken's soft sexy chuckle filled Greg's mind. The familiar sound helped Greg relax, but he wanted answers soon. *"And you'll get them, but not right this moment."* Ken's voice in his head addressed his concerns. *"Now, go get your pistol. You're probably going to need it real soon. Also get Casey into the cabin. He'll be safer there."*

* * *

Greg called Casey to him, hurried into the cabin, and soon reappeared alone. He moved with a stiffness Ken had come to associate with him having his pistol in the back waistband of his jeans.

The black van emerged from the trees and picked up speed.

Greg's pulse increased, Ken could feel it through the telepathic link he'd established. He also caught flashes of someone important being shot. *"That looks like the van that ambushed us in the alley."*

Ken tried to push out calming emotions. He wasn't about to let anything untold happen to Greg. They were getting along great and he was going to keep Greg alive at any costs. *"When you got shot?"*

"Yeah." Greg's hands balled into fists, and his right one eased back to his hip, ready to draw his gun.

* * *

A black SUV, that looked like a black ops government van, completely devoid of any markings, roared into the clearing and came to a stop in a puff of powdery snow. Greg gasped as Kyle Hudson and two strangers got out. All three wore uniforms. The two strangers looked to be from the FBI and the Portland Fire Department. This seemed as unreal as Ken just vanishing in front of him.

Greg's head spun in shock. He put a hand against the cabin wall to steady himself. Hudson was one of the men he and the captain trusted the most. He couldn't believe Hudson was dirty. But if he was there at the cabin, there wasn't any other explanation. The other men with him just confirmed his guilt, and solidified Greg's growing concerns that the leak in their department might be a lot more than just a police level problem. The lack of an easily-found money trail had sparked that question in his mind.

Hudson waved. "Hi, Greg." He looked and sounded like nothing was amiss.

Greg took a deep breath and forced himself to be calm. Ken was there with him, even if he couldn't see him. "What are you doing here, Kyle, and who are those two?"

A wide grin spread across Hudson's face, but the smile didn't reach his eyes. "Captain sent me to check on you. Thought you might need something before winter sets in." He motioned to the two men. "These are a couple of new guys the commissioner sent to help with the work load since the other two didn't work out."

"What happened to Adams and Murphy? And why are these guys dressed the way they are? Why aren't they in regular uniforms?" He hoped he got the names of the replacements right. He'd only met them once. Greg reached out to Ken. *I've been in contact with the captain. He didn't say anything about new recruits or sending anyone up here.*

"Don't worry." Ken replied. It was impossible to tell how close he was, but somehow his thoughts were enough to help Greg feel safer. *"I've got this. Whatever you do, don't let them into the cabin. I won't be able to help inside."*

"They didn't work out. Adams is a drunk and Whitaker reported Murphy for sexual harassment. Couldn't keep his hands off of her." Hudson snorted. "Not that I blame him. She's a looker. I wouldn't mind a piece of that myself." He stepped closer to Greg. "As to the uniforms, the commissioner thought we needed some outside help. They just got transferred today."

Greg seethed inside at the cavalier way he spoke of Whitaker. It was totally out of character for the Hudson he thought he knew. "But the fire department, and what's the guy in the suit?"

"He's FBI. They stepped in because this operation seems to be in more than just Oregon. The fire department was called in because we've had some arson attacks. You do remember your house burning down, don't you?"

Hudson had what sounded like a plausible answer for everything.

Something shimmered between Greg and Hudson, and the three men looked distorted.

"Hey, what happened?" Hudson asked. "There's something between us." He stepped forward and came to an abrupt stop. "I ran into something." He put out his hands and moved them like he was touching an object. "He's got someone out here protecting him!"

Greg remembered what Ken said about not acting surprised by anything, but he wondered how Hudson knew he was being protected by someone, and what they were touching. He couldn't wait to get Ken alone and dig out he answers.

"Tell him it's a force field."

"It's a force field. I learned how to project it for protection." Greg grinned, he wondered if he sounded as crazy as he thought he did. *"Where are you?"*

"I'm right in front of you, baby. I'm the force field." Ken chuckled. "Hey, that tickles."

Hudson's hand kept moving in the air. "It's something warm and scaly. It feels like a giant snake, except snakes are cold." He tried to look around the distortion. "What makes you think you need protection from me?"

"Because I've been in contact with the captain. He didn't say anything about sending someone up here, or about any more arson cases or the FBI." He tilted his head and squinted. "Looks to me like we know who the leak in the department is."

"What makes you think it's me and not the captain?" Hudson huffed.

Greg shook his head. He moved slightly to keep the shimmer between him and the others. His gut told him he was safer that way. "Because the captain has known for weeks where I am. He arranged for me to be here. If he wanted to, he could have been here a long time ago."

The two strangers drew their guns and moved toward Greg about three feet to the right of Hudson. They also came to an abrupt stop when they ran into the obstacle.

The guy in the fire department uniform dropped his gun and grabbed his wrist. His palm had red welts starting to well up on it. "Something made my gun hot. It burned my hand."

The FBI agent threw his weapon on the ground and jumped away from it. "What's happening? It's like my gun's on fire. Damn it, I hate magic. Hudson, we're not prepared for this. The boss didn't say anything about dealing with magic!"

"I don't know." Hudson looked confused. "I've never heard of Williams having any magical abilities."

"I need to let out some steam. I'm getting heartburn." Two streams of fire burst from about twenty feet in the air and hit the van causing it to explode.

The blast knocked the three men over.

"Hope you have some rope, Greg."

"I think there's some in the shed." Greg turned and ran for the small building ignoring the twitch in his knee, and thankful for the knee brace that made him a lot more stable.

"I'll hold them while you get it."

The rope was right where he thought it should be and he was heading back in a flash with it. With the adrenaline coursing through him, he was just reacting in the most logical fashion he could. He was worried that if he stopped to analyze what was happening his mind might rebel, no matter what he'd been told.

As he reached the men on the ground, his attackers were beginning to struggle, but they looked like they all had invisible anvils holding them to the ground.

"Hey, something's on top of me." Hudson beat at something on his chest. "It weighs a ton."

"My tail isn't that heavy. Or maybe it is. I know altogether I weigh about two tons."

"What are you?" Greg had lots of questions filling his head, but he wanted to wait until they could speak like normal people. The telepathy was weirding him out a bit. It felt odd.

The other two were also struggling. The FBI guy shimmered and for a moment looked like he was going to turn to liquid, then he solidified.

"Oh, that's interesting." Ken muttered.

"What?" Greg wasn't sure what he'd just seen. But it was all so strange, he wasn't sure what was causing any of it.

"Something strange is happening with these guys."

"You think it's strange? What about what I'm thinking?" Greg was quickly reaching his limit of strange. He wanted answers, not more questions. If Hudson and his friends were part of the Black Fins, how far did the corruption go? The things he'd been working on for months were easier to think about than the strangeness happening right before his eyes. None of that made any sense.

"I think they may be some kind of shifter."

"It feels like a big snake," FBI guy yelled

"Feels to me like a tail of some kind," the fireman shouted. "I can't budge it."

Greg returned with a hank of rope. *"How do I tie them when I can't see what's holding them down."* He had no idea how to get their hands and feet together. He might be able to just lift them up and make a hog tie around whatever was holding them down, but he wasn't sure that would work.

"Guess this is as good a time as any. Greg, please *don't freak out on me. If you do, we might both be lost. These men are more than just men."*

A huge silver-colored dragon appeared above the men. It looked down at Hudson with a dangerous gleam in its glimmering green eyes. The eyes were Ken's eyes, and the dragon was the same color as Ken's hair.

Hudson screamed. "It's going to eat me."

Greg's eyes opened wide as he stared amazed at the creature in front of him. What was this? A dragon? He'd known Ken for almost a month. Why hadn't he told him what he was? Maybe this was what Bob had talked about to the captain the previous month. No time to wonder. He had to tie the men up.

"Tell him I don't eat rotten cops." Ken's tone was sour. He lifted the end of his tail so Greg could tie Hudson.

Greg grinned and repeated Ken's words. As he rolled Hudson over, pulled his arms behind him, and wrapped the rope around them, two police cars came roaring into the clearing.

"Be sure he's tied tight. Wrap the rope around his arms and secure them to his body. If he's a shifter, that will keep him from changing."

The captain and Whitaker jumped out of one and Carter and Adams out of the other.

Greg tied Hudson's wrists and ankles together, and then followed Ken's instructions to wrap the rope so his arms were held close to his body.

"What happened here?" The captain looked up at the head of the silvery-colored dragon with its tail draped over the last two men. "Williams?" His voice was a mix of wonder and fear.

Greg shook his head. "Don't ask me, Captain. Ask the dragon." He wasn't sure why his mind wasn't a gibbering mess of crazy, but he understood Ken was the dragon and he trusted him just as he had since the first day they met. It just would've been nice to be let in on the secret though. They'd gotten so close and shared so much already. He would demand an explanation later.

Carter looked up at Ken's head and swallowed with a loud gulp. "Dragons don't exist."

Greg chuckled. "Tell that to him." He nodded toward the dragon.

"You could introduce me. My name in this form is Kynth. I'm a platinum dragon, and am over a thousand years old. I've lived in this area for the last five hundred years."

Greg repeated what Kynth had said.

Hudson yelled, "Don't let him eat me, Captain."

Carter leaned over and slapped his thigh laughing.

"It isn't funny, Carter." Hudson shouted. "See how *you* feel with a dragon's tail on top of you. He's going to eat me. I know he is." Like the FBI guy had done before him, Hudson's form blurred and for a second it looked like his fingers were merging into something different, but the tight ropes held his arms so he couldn't move. Then he shook and lay still.

Carter chuckled again. "I just remembered a bumper sticker I saw once. *Do not meddle in the affairs of dragons, for you are crunchy and taste good with ketchup.* Hey, dragon, want some ketchup?"

"Ask him if I should eat him raw or roast him first." Kynth raised his nose into the air and blew two flames upward. *"I don't know how much you want to tell your friends, but these men are also more than they appear. I'm not exactly sure yet, but we need to be careful. Bind them tightly; they can't change if they're bound."*

"What do you mean?" Greg asked as he repeated Kynth's question out loud, Hudson screamed again, and a noxious stench filled the air. It reminded Greg of the chum he'd smelled on some of the fishing boats in the harbor.

"These men aren't human. Their human skin is just a disguise." Kynth said.

Whitaker pinched her nose. "Whew. Smells a little rotten there. Don't think I'd want to eat it."

"Like yours is?" Greg suddenly realized he'd been having sex with someone very different from himself even if Ken looked human at the time of their encounters.

"Yes and no. We'll talk about me later." Kynth turned to Whitaker, lowered his head, and blinked as he bobbed his head several times in rapid succession.

"You can bet on that. You have a lot of questions to answer." There was no way Greg was going to let Ken off the hook without answering his questions.

"He's laughing." She reached up and placed her hand on his nose. "Aren't you, dragon?"

Kynth bobbed his head and rubbed against her hand.

"Do you want to come home with me? My kids would love it."

"Your husband probably wouldn't," Greg told her. He was still wrestling with trying to figure exactly what was happening with all this and she was accepting everything like it was just another part of her day to day life. He wondered how mentally stable she was, then he wondered how stable *he* was. There was too much going on. He studied Whitaker for a moment, trying to figure out if she was more than she let on and that's why she was being so accepting of Ken's differences.

Kynth turned and looked at Greg. *"You know, if you'd finish tying these guys up, I could move."*

"Sorry, I got distracted." "Whitaker, give me your handcuffs. Carter you cuff the one on the end."

"Don't forget to immobilize their arms so they can't change."

Greg and Carter worked quickly. There was something refreshing about being able to cuff someone again.

The FBI guy tried to punch Greg as Kynth let up on him. Greg dodged the blow, and the man got to his feet and ran for the lake. Kynth moved faster, and put a taloned claw down on top of him before he got more than three steps.

"I don't think we want them getting to the water." Kynth said as Greg grabbed hold of the man and hauled him to his feet.

"Think they could get away then? We've got them cuffed." Greg forced the FBI guy toward Carter and the fireman.

"Maybe. With the odor that came from Hudson a while ago, I think they may be some kind of fish."

When the three had been secured to the porch railing, the dragon shrank and became human.

"Captain, Carter, Whitaker, meet Ken Draig." Greg took Ken's hand. He felt like he always did. Warmer than the normal person, but still the large strong hands that held Greg each night. For a moment, it was as if nothing had changed. "Like Bob said, things aren't always what they seem to be."

"Whoa, Greg." Whitaker looked at Ken with eyes almost more wide than she had Kynth. "You were right. My husband wouldn't want me to bring that home."

Ken smiled and winked at her.

Greg looked at the captain. "So what made you come up here today?"

"Hudson said his sister had an accident." He nodded toward Whitaker. "Whitaker remembered he'd her told a few years ago that he's an only child and both parents are dead. I got suspicious. I tried calling, but your cell phone just went to voice mail."

Greg shrugged. "Glad you did." He'd never been so happy to see the captain as he had been when they piled out of the cars. Somehow it helped put the strangeness of Ken being a dragon into the real world. He still wanted to sit and talk to Ken about it, then he had a lot of thinking to do. "I thought you knew about the spotty cell service up this way."

"I do." The captain walked over to the three prisoners. "Now, we need to figure out who Hudson's friends are, and how they found out about you being up here."

"What have you got in mind, Captain?" Greg asked as he leaned against the squad car and glared at the men bound to the porch. "Are they under arrest?"

"No, to be perfectly honest, we're out of our jurisdiction up here." The captain rubbed his chin and started pacing between the cars and the house. "We're in the middle of the Mount Hood National Forest. That's federal." He paused and stared at the FBI guy. "I bet your friends would get you out of anything I put you up for in a heartbeat. That is if they know what you're up to."

The man stared at Captain Wood but didn't say anything.

Captain Wood stomped over to Hudson. "But you, Hudson"—He sighed—"you're a bigger problem to me. Your betrayal cost Jackson his life. Don't think I've forgotten about that."

"You don't know what you're messing with here, Captain!" Hudson shouted. "This is bigger than all of you." He laughed. "We're bigger than all of you, except the dragon. The boss won't be very happy to learn about a dragon living up here. I didn't think there were any dragons in North America."

Ken growled deep in his throat. The sound sent shivers up and down Greg's spine. He knew beyond a doubt, Ken didn't want a lot of people knowing he was up there.

"And who is your boss, Hudson?" Captain Wood grabbed Hudson by the hair. "You might want to tell us, or we might think about feeding you to the dragon. But somehow, I bet a few small fry like yourselves won't make a very good meal for him."

"I'd rather not." Ken stayed where he was, leaning next to Greg on the cruiser, but he'd gotten noticeably tense.

The captain gestured between the captives and Ken. "See, he's a nice dragon. He'd rather not have to eat you. But we've got to do something with the three of you. You've all got valuable information we need."

"Then we have a problem," the FBI man said. "We're not about to start talking. There's nothing you can do to us that going to scare us. You're all weak."

"Weak." The captain's voice took on a low dangerous tone. "Let's see who's weak." He pulled out his service pistol and shot the FBI guy in the knee cap.

Greg winced. He knew the pain the man was in. If it hadn't been for Jackson's death, he would've objected to the captain's actions, but he wanted to find out who was at the center of their problems. Who was pulling the Black Fins' strings?

The FBI guy screamed, then started laughing. "Is that they best you've got?"

"I hadn't expected them to show their hand this quickly." Ken's thoughts entered Greg's mind.

"What?" Greg glanced at Ken and then at the wounded prisoner.

There was the odd shimmer again, but this time it was just centered on the man's leg.

"What just happened?" Whitaker hurried over and ripped the man's pants where the bullet entered. She back peddled, staring at him. "What are you?"

The FBI guy laughed again and looked at Ken. "We're not dragons. But we're close. Very close."

Ken shook his head. "Captain Wood. I believe your justice system won't be able to safely provide these men with the incarceration they require without a little help from me."

"What?" The captain holstered his gun and walked over to the cruiser and looked from Greg to Ken. "Do you have any ideas? What are these guys?"

"Exactly? I don't know." Ken crossed his arms and looked toward the porch like he was trying to see through something. "But they aren't human. They're shifters of some kind."

Greg blinked. "Shifters? Shape shifters? Like the books you write? Like you?"

Ken shook his head. "Not like me. But yes to the other questions."

With a sigh, the captain turned back to the prisoners. "And how are we supposed to hold shifters?"

"Captain. I don't think this falls into our job description," Carter spoke up from where he sat on the trunk of the second cruiser. "We enforce human laws. If these guys aren't human, even though they look it, they're breaking human laws." He shrugged.

"They still deserve to face justice for what they've done," Whitaker snapped. "We just can't kill them off the cuff. As much as they deserve it."

"Plus we don't know who they're working with. We don't know who controls the Black Fins. Hudson can't be the only leak in the department." Greg stomped over to stand next to the captain where he studied the three. "Hudson wouldn't have had the clout to pull the blockade off the alley that night. That came from higher up." That was one thing he'd been able to figure out in his research since he'd been up the mountain. The call that pulled the second SWAT team off had come from someone who knew the codes to bypass dispatch and get directly to them. There wasn't anything on the official record about the call. That was suspicious on its own.

"He hasn't liked you poking around," the fireman spoke up. "Humans who get to close to us, end up like your partner. He was getting too close and had to be eliminated. We tried to eliminate you too." He thrashed around and the porch railing creaked.

"Oh no you don't." Ken moved in a blaze of speed and hit the man in the forehead.

The fireman stopped struggling and hung limp, his handcuffs suspending him on the rail.

"Did you kill him?" Whitaker asked, dashing over to feel the man's neck.

Ken shook his head. "No. Just a little tap to put him out." He looked at the other two. "Now, are you two going to talk, or do I need to resort to more direct methods to get information out of you?"

"All you could do is kill us, dragon!" Hudson spat on the ground at Ken's feet. "If you don't kill us, he will if we talk. We're not going to betray anyone."

With a heavy sigh, Ken turned to Captain Wood. "It's your call, Captain."

"What can we do?" the captain asked. "If they can heal bullet wounds..."

"There are several ways to kill most shifters." Ken glanced back over his shoulder. "I doubt these two will be able to withstand everything I know about that."

Greg walked over and stared at Hudson. He'd known the man—he guessed he could still call him a man—for years. "Have you been hiding all this time, Kyle?"

"Why do you care?" Hudson responded without lifting his eyes. "You're going to be dead soon. We were just the first wave. There will be more of us coming for you. And they'll keep coming until you're dead."

"No they won't." Ken put a hand on Greg's shoulder. His warmth hit just the right spot and made Greg feel secure.

Greg wished he could lean into Ken, like they did when they sat on the couch watching movies as the snow fell outside. But it wasn't the time for accepting comfort, plus Ken still had a lot of questions to answer. He wasn't going to get comfortable with Ken again until they spent a lot of time talking.

"I'm not going to let them harm anyone else," Ken continued. "Greg Williams and the other humans of the Portland Police Department are now under my protection."

No response came from the men.

The silence lingered.

"Looks like they're afraid of you," Carter said. "I guess that's something."

"Yes it is." Ken walked up to Hudson. "Now that I've got your attention. Maybe you can tell me about your superior. Who sent you after Greg?"

A large wet spot appeared on the front of Hudson's slacks. "I can't. He'll kill all of us."

"Shut up, fool!" the FBI guy snapped.

"No, please,"—Ken ran a finger across Hudson's face—"keep talking. Tell me what I need to know. I'll see you get safe passage to wherever you want to go."

Greg didn't like the sound of that. "Ken, Hudson has to pay for what he did. He has to stand trial."

"You still don't get it, Williams." Hudson looked over Ken's shoulder and sneered. "There won't be any trial for me, for any of us. We're beyond your human laws. We're just trying to regain what's ours."

"And what is yours?" Ken took hold of Hudson's chin and jerked his gaze away from Greg.

"This land. Everything here. It belonged to us long before the whites came. The natives knew how to respect us. How to share the land with us, but the whites don't."

Captain Wood scratched his head. "What's he going on about? He's as white as the rest of us. And what does the land have to do with a gang who runs drugs? This doesn't make sense."

"And it's not going to." The FBI guy jerked on his handcuffs, snapping the metal. He shoved Ken aside and rammed his hand into Hudson's chest.

"Shit!" Carter pulled his gun and he and Adams opened fire.

Thirty rounds of lead slammed into the FBI's guy's back as he snapped the fireman's neck. He jerked with each round, then fell to the ground.

"Damn it!" Captain Wood made it to the porch in record time. "We were just getting somewhere."

Ken stood and dusted off his jeans. "I can't believe he took me by surprise. That shouldn't have happened."

"What were they?" Captain Wood turned on Ken. "You said they weren't human. Hudson wasn't talking like a human would."

Ken shook his head. "I don't know. They died in their human forms. We'll never know. It's not like I can just look at a shifter and know what they are. It doesn't work that way."

"And what are we going to do with the bodies?" Greg asked. He wasn't looking forward to having three frozen corpses on his porch until spring thaw. And if that happened, he'd let the captain explain it to Bob.

Whitaker looked puzzled. "How did the bullets kill him? When the captain shot him, his knee wasn't even injured."

"In their other form, the bullets wouldn't have fazed him. Like when I'm in dragon form, bullets pretty much bounce off. But in human form, if a bullet hits a vital organ like the heart or brain, it would kill me. As many bullets as hit him, at least one of them had to have hit something important." He turned to the captain. "With your permission, I can take care of the bodies. My dragon fire can cremate them just as well as a crematorium. Then you can scatter their ashes around and no one will ever know what happened to them."

The Black Fin Case

The captain nodded his approval.

Chapter Twelve

ONCE KYNTH had burned the bodies and the captain and others were gone, Greg stormed around the cabin. He didn't know whether to be angry or hurt. He was just glad he'd managed to hold things together until everyone left. "Just when did you intend to tell me I've been sleeping with a dragon for the last month?" He sat on the couch and threw one of the pillows across the room. "A dragon! Like something out of a fairy tale. Dragons don't exist."

"Calm down, Greg. I can assure you I exist. I've just been trying to find the words to tell you what I am." Ken leaned against the mantel. "It isn't easy. It's been a long time since I told anyone except Bob. Most of the men I'm with, I haven't cared enough about to reveal myself to."

Greg stood, walked over to the pillow, and picked it up. He might be upset, but he didn't want to have to pick things up later. "So is that what Bob meant by, 'things aren't always what they seem'?"

Ken shrugged. "I'm not sure what he meant."

"You said you're a thousand years old?" He sat in the chair with his arms around the throw pillow. He was okay with older men, but a thousand years old was a lot different from sixty.

"Give or take a few." Ken scratched his head. "I know I was born before the Normans took over England."

"I'm trying to understand this. Really, I am." Greg tossed the pillow back on the couch, stood, and paced across the room. He did his best to reign in the anger and focus on the questions he had. As a detective, questions were part of his job. If he could get questions out and get honest answers for them, he'd feel better about things. "You're from England? So why do you live in a cabin in the wilds of Oregon?"

"I'm not really from England. I'm from Wales."

That didn't exactly make sense. "Isn't Wales part of England?"

"Yes and no. It's part of the United Kingdom, and is ruled by the queen. However, it is a separate country. Also, I don't live in a cabin in Oregon."

Greg glared at him. The answer sounded like a riddle, or something more obtuse. "The day we met, you said you live in a cabin across the cove. Was that a lie?"

Ken slowly shook his head. "I said I *have* a cabin across the cove. I don't live there. It's just where I write."

"Okay, let's take this one thing at a time." Greg wanted to roll his eyes, trying to understand how they were actually having the strange conversation they were having. It didn't make a whole lot of sense. He held his hands in front of him palms down. "Where do you live?"

"I have a lair in a cave up on Mt. Hood." He gestured at the wall in approximately the direction of the mountain. "It's just below the tree line on the west side of the mountain. I've been there since before Oregon became a state. When I want to sleep in dragon form, it's where I go."

That didn't make a whole lot of sense, other than in all the legends, dragons lived in caves. "Isn't it dangerous? What about an eruption?"

"I was there when it erupted in 1866. Had to leave for a while." Ken walked across the floor toward him. "Greg, does any of this really matter?"

"I thought I was getting to know you. I know I've developed feelings for you." Holding up a hand to fend off Ken, Greg shook his head. He didn't want Ken coming in and touching him at that moment. He needed distance to remain objective. "Now I find out you're some weird creature that isn't supposed to exist. I don't know what to believe. I think you'd better leave." He pointed to the door and willed himself not to give in to the feelings that were cascading around in his brain. He wanted Ken to hold him but he also wanted time to sort everything out. He wasn't sure he'd be able to make a life with a dragon. It sounded so strange.

"When you're ready to talk, I'll be back." Ken walked over and tried to touch Greg's face.

Greg pulled back. He swallowed hard and crossed his arms. "Just go." The adrenaline of the earlier danger was gone. He needed space and time to sort out his feelings.

* * *

On his flight from his cave the next morning, Kynth was surprised to see the signal flag flying from the corner of Greg's porch. He landed in the yard and found Greg sitting on the porch with a stricken look on his face.

Without a word, Greg stood and ran to Ken as he shifted, burying his face on his shoulder.

"What's wrong?" Ken stroked Greg's hair. This hadn't been how he'd hoped they would reconnect. But he was willing to take what he could. If Greg needed him for comfort, there was hope for them. He'd had a rough night worrying about Greg. It had been the first night they'd spent apart in two weeks.

"Carter's dead." Greg's voice broke and he shook.

Alarmed, Ken pulled back and looked into Greg's eyes. "What? What happened? Did they have an accident?"

"No accident, but they're not really sure yet what happened." Greg shook his head and collapsed back against Ken's shoulder. "The captain called. When Carter and Adams didn't show up at the precinct, the captain and Whitaker backtracked looking for them. They found the car with Carter's body just the other side of Government Camp.

He'd been shot execution style with a bullet to the back of the head. It looked like he was shot with his own gun. It was lying next to his body."

It worried Ken. The previous day, more humans found out about his existence than had known in a hundred years. As long as he thought it was just the police, he hadn't been too alarmed. But this was different. If it got to the wrong ears, it could be disastrous. He might have to go into hiding somewhere other than Oregon. Maybe even go back to Wales. "What about Adams?"

Greg shook his head again. "No sign of him. There were tire tracks in the snow where another vehicle was next to the police car. A pile of cigarette butts made it look like the other car was waiting for them."

Ken brushed Greg's hair back off of his forehead. "Does the captain think Adams was in on it?"

"He said it looks that way." Greg stepped out of Ken's arms and started pacing on the porch. "Would that mean Murphy's in on it too? Are they working together?"

"Have they been in the department long?" Ken stepped out of his way, but wanted to take Greg back into his arms and provide what comfort he could.

Greg sighed. "Not at all. In fact, they've only been there a few weeks. The commissioner sent them in when the captain asked for help ferreting out the leak. They were replacements for Jackson and me." He moved toward the door. "I need more coffee. I'm having trouble thinking straight."

Ken followed him into the cabin. "What does the captain think you should do?" He glanced at the couch which was pulled out and hadn't been made. That was a major statement to Greg's state of mind. Except for the first few days he was at the cabin, he always made the bed.

Greg filled his cup and reached for another one for Ken. "He wants me to stay here and lie low."

"What do you want?" Ken took his cup and smelled it. Greg made an excellent cup of coffee. When he stopped to think about it, Greg was an overall good cook. But as a long-term bachelor, he probably had to be, or be at the mercy of fast food, and Greg didn't have the body of someone who ate a lot of fast food.

"They already know where I am." He sipped his drink. "I feel like a sitting duck out here alone."

Ken smiled at him. He didn't bother adding they also knew about him and the odds were they'd up the ante to either take him out of the game or get him on their side. Shifters could be like that some times. "You aren't alone. I'm here." He moved to the couch and folded it up without straightening the bedding. "Let's sit down and think this out."

Once Greg settled beside him and pulled his legs up on the couch, Ken placed his arm around Greg's shoulders. Casey sat between them and put his head on Ken's knee with a soft whine for petting. He flashed back to the number of times they'd sat on the couch watching movies and making out. They had more serious things to work out in that moment, but it was still nice to have Greg beside him, particularly after the way they'd left things the previous night. "So what do you think you should do?"

Greg leaned against Ken. It felt right. "I feel I should be back in town. Maybe I'll see something someone else might miss."

Ken lifted his head and turned toward the door. There was something coming toward them. It roared down the narrow road through the cramped passage between the trees. The sound was unmistakable. Trouble was barreling right at them.

"We have to get out of here. Grab Casey." He stood and hurried toward the door. He was going to have to act fast, or lives were going to be lost. He couldn't stand losing Greg and he was fairly fond of Casey too. "Come on. No time to lose."

Greg followed Ken outside as the dog bounced along with them.

"Give me Casey and put your arms around me from the back." The sound of the vehicle was getting closer. He couldn't be sure what it was, but if Greg had spoken to the captain that morning and received the news about Carter, it wasn't going to be the good guys.

"What's going on?" Greg picked up Casey and the dog squirmed in his hands.

"No time for questions. Just do what I say and we'll all be okay." Ken took Casey, removed his belt, and looped it around the dog's middle and through his collar forming a makeshift harness. He held Casey close to his chest. "Quiet, Casey. I can't have you wiggling or barking."

Casey raised his head and licked Ken's face.

Greg did as Ken said and hugged him from behind.

Ken shifted.

Ridges sprung out of his back and wings spread on each side of Greg right behind his legs.

Casey whined and thrashed in Ken's grip, but his claws were large enough to encompass the dog, the belt through his collar gave Ken a place to hold onto without injuring him.

Soon Greg was lying on the back of the dragon. "Ouch. What's happening? You almost mangled my family jewels."

"Sorry about that. Scoot forward until one of the ridges is at your back and hold on to the one just in front of you." It had been a very long time since he'd had anyone on his back. Greg's weight felt strange and if he'd been a little bit larger, it would've been awkward.

"What about Casey?"

"I have Casey. Don't worry about him. Just watch the road."

A black SUV identical to the previous one, came into view.

"They'll see us."

"Didn't you learn anything yesterday?"

"You may be invisible, but what about me and Casey?"

Ken resisted a chuckle. *"As long as you're part of me, you're also invisible. Just hold on tight."*

Adams and two other men got out of the van and walked up on the porch carrying assault rifles. Ken wondered how many people were involved with the Black Fins. It was looking like there was a fair number of them. They were definitely more than a large gang just running drugs. That made him wonder more about Hudson's ranting about taking the land back. Were there enough men around who weren't exactly men to do that? Were any normal humans safe?

Adams looked in the open door. "It looks like he's gone."

One of the other men went into the cabin and called back. "He left in a hurry. The coffee pot's still hot, and there are two cups on the table. Anyone want a cup?"

"We don't have time for that." Adams pulled a cell phone from his pocket and dialed. "He's gone. He hasn't been gone long, and his car is still here. He's probably in the woods somewhere. No sign of the dragon either." After listening to the person on the other end, he ended the call and said, "Jennings says to torch the place and his car and then see if we can track him."

"If it's a fire they want, I think I'll help them along." Kynth blew two streams of fire at the front porch.

"Are we flying?" Greg's heart rate soared and his legs tightened around Kynth's neck as his muscles bunched and his wings moved.

"Have to keep moving so they can't find us." Kynth headed out over the lake. He felt safer with more distance between them and the guns.

One of the men on the porch screamed as the fire caught his pants. "That dragon must be here!"

The second man ran out of the cabin with his gun in firing position. "Where is he?" He fired the rifle in a low arc across the yard.

"Now see why I took to the air?" Kynth hoped they wouldn't try a similar shooting tactic higher up. He might not be able to protect Greg and Casey if they did that.

Adams ran off the porch.

"I hope there's nothing in there that's important to you."

"I lost everything when they burned my house. Other than my grandmother's quilt and the carvings I've been doing since I've been up here, you're holding the only thing important to me. I can replace the carvings. I'm sure Grandma will understand the loss of the quilt. I hope you have a good hold on Casey."

There was a tightness in Greg's words, and Kynth wanted to fly down and rescue the quilt, but it was too dangerous for all of them. He'd started the fire with dragon fire. It could damage him.

"I do, and he's being very cooperative and quiet." When they'd gained some altitude Casey had remarkably calmed. It was making things easier.

"Can he hear our thoughts?"

"He can hear. Not sure how much he understands." The idea of communicating telepathically with animals was something the dragons had debated almost as much as humans debated simply talking to them.

Kynth turned around until he was again facing the cabin and sent two streams of flame to the roof. *"Hope Bob forgives me for burning down his cabin."*

"You or them. Does it matter who starts the fire? I just thought of something. Adams said, 'Jennings'. You don't suppose he meant the police commissioner do you? If he did, this thing is even bigger than we thought. Jennings would've been able to call off the SWAT team at the alley the night Jackson died."

As the three men ran for their SUV, Kynth torched it. They turned toward Greg's Explorer. But Kynth was faster than they were. Two of the men looked fairly damaged when the Explorer blew up as they approached it. It would take them a while to recover unless they were able to shift.

"That'll leave them on foot." Kynth circled the clearing, making sure the flames didn't spread to the trees and get into the forest. He didn't want to be responsible for setting the Mount Hood National Forest on fire. It would take too long for it to regrow. *"Do you want to hang around, or should we head for the city?"*

Greg sighed. *"I think I need to contact the captain as soon as possible."*

"Okay."

Kynth flew across the cove and lit in a clearing beside an A-frame cabin a bit larger than Bob's. As he landed, he became human.

* * *

Greg's feet touched the ground and he fell to his knees. The impact jarred his knee, but it wasn't nearly as bad as it would've been a few weeks earlier. "That was quite a ride. Never dreamed I'd ride a dragon." The impact of what he'd just done hit him, and his head spun a bit. He wanted to stay there in the snow until he felt more stable, but he had things to do. He stood.

"Baby, you've been riding me for a few weeks now." Ken set Casey on the ground, pulled Greg into his arms, and kissed him.

Greg tilted his head and glared. "That's a bit different type of riding." Anger was easier, but he wanted to have time to let Ken know how great it was for him to come flying in and rescue him. Ken made him feel safe. No matter what else they were going through, Ken had quickly become a safe person for Greg, someone he wanted to be with for the rest of his life.

Casey ran around the new area sniffing and peeing.

Greg patted his pockets. "Damn."

"What's wrong?"

"I left that cell phone in the cabin." He wasn't going to be able to let the captain know what was going on.

"It's toast now. Here, use mine."

Greg dialed the number of the precinct.

"Officer Whitaker. How can I help you?" Her cheerful voice sounded out of place for the morning he was having.

"Morning, Whitaker." Somehow, her cheerfulness felt out of place for the morning he was having. "I need to talk to the captain."

"Williams, is that you? Are you okay?"

"Let me talk to Wood. I'll explain things to him." It was all he could do to not be snappy. She'd done nothing to deserve his anger, but at that point anger was the strongest emotion he had.

She placed him on hold.

"Wood."

Greg let out the breath he hadn't realize he was holding as he waited for his superior to pick up. "Captain?"

"Williams, what are you doing calling here, and whose phone are you on? You're supposed to maintain silence."

"Can't talk. Your phone may be bugged. Meet me at the usual place in. . . ." He turned to Ken. "How long will it take?"

Ken looked thoughtful for a moment. "Just over an hour."

Greg nodded. "Okay, Captain. I'll be there in about an hour and a half." He was giving them a little extra time in case of problems.

"See you then, but you'd better have a good reason."

"I do." He dropped his voice, even though he knew if the line was bugged the people listening would be able to up his volume when they replayed the recording. "Don't tell anyone. And I mean anyone, not Whitaker, not Strader, not Stevens, and especially not Murphy."

"Got it."

"You might want to send someone out to see if they can find Adams, and those other two guys. We left them at Bob's burned out cabin with two non-drivable cars. A couple of them might need medical attention, so tell them to take their time." At that point, Greg didn't care if the men bled out while waiting for help or not. They'd done enough to piss him off, and they weren't human anyway. From what they saw of Hudson and the others they were fairly hardy. Adams and the two with him might already be healed and headed back to town.

"Burned? What happened?"

"Tell you when we see you." Greg ended the call, reflexively put the phone in his pocket and turned to Ken. He was ready to go. The faster they got to town, the sooner they'd get everything sorted out. He was afraid of someone, or something, warning Jennings before they got there. The commissioner could either set up an ambush, or run, depending on how much they really had on him and the Black Fins. "Let's do this."

"I'll be right back." Ken went into the cabin and came out carrying a sheet and some leather straps. "I think Casey'll do better with you holding him. Wrap this around him like a sling. Just don't drop him. I don't want to have to dive after him." He fastened the leather around himself, and kissed Greg. "When I morph, put your feet in the stirrups and hold on."

Greg called Casey and picked him up. "Hold on, boy. We're going for another dragon ride." He placed the sheet around Casey and tied it around his waist and neck like a baby sling, leaned against Ken's back with a squirming Casey between them, and was soon once again on the back of the dragon. As they circled the lake once, gaining altitude, Greg glanced down and could've sworn he saw three large black fins cutting across the lake toward the river that would take them toward the Pacific Ocean. He was surprised by the size of the fins. He'd lived in Oregon all of his life and never heard of fish that big in a fresh-water lake. Then they were over the trees and all water was gone. He wished he had some goggles to help with the wind that lashed at his eyes. In his grasp, Casey whined and buried his nose under the sheet. Then Kynth was moving so fast, Greg had to close his eyes and miss the spectacle of the trip down the mountain at just above tree level.

Just over an hour later, Kynth landed in the parking lot of Paco's Tacos. He morphed into human and looked around. "You can't take Casey inside. I'll stay out here with him."

"Okay." Greg leaned in for a quick kiss, handed over the dog, and stepped away. He instantly became visible and hoped no one was watching. It would be hard to explain to most people.

Inside the restaurant, the captain was already waiting for him. He walked in and sat in the booth across from him.

"I hope you haven't been bugged." Greg said, resisting the urge to pick up the hot sauce bottle and start playing with it. "This thing is a lot bigger than we thought. Commissioner Jennings may be part of it."

"What makes you think that? I had a meeting with Jennings this morning. He thinks members of the Black Fins kidnapped Adams after they killed Carter." He looked about. His gaze darting around like he was making sure he could recognize everyone in the restaurant.

The waitress approached and Captain Wood held up a hand, "Just bring us coffee."

She nodded and left.

"Did you question the fact that Commissioner Jennings sent a dirty cop into the precinct?" Greg pulled a couple of sugar packets out of the display in anticipation of the coffee. It also gave him something to do with his hands. "Murphy's probably dirty also."

The captain frowned. "You think Jennings knows Adams is dirty?"

"I know he does." Greg tapped the sugar packets, hoping he didn't hit one of them too hard and make a mess on the table. "Adams called him from the cabin. Jennings told him to torch the cabin, and then try to track me in the woods."

Captain Wood raised his eyebrows as his frown deepened. "How did you escape?"

Greg grinned. "On the back of a fire-breathing dragon." If he had to admit it, his adrenaline was still surging after the ride into town. It had been the coolest thing he'd ever done. Somehow it was a start in Ken making up for keeping his secret for so long.

"That must have been some ride."

"It was. Oh, you'd better call Bob about the burned cabin. Ken apologized, but if he hadn't burned it, Adams was going to." Greg didn't want to go into the pain he felt at the loss of everything he owned for the second time in as many months. It wasn't fair. He'd done everything he could to be a good cop and keep his community safe, and he was left with a burned-down family house and the loss of the little bit he'd replaced since then. But at least he, Casey, and Ken were alright. The fact he thought of Ken reminded him how close they'd grown in a short while.

"What do you suggest we do?" The captain tapped the table.

"Let me back in the field." Out of the corner of his eye, he watched a car park next to the café.

The driver got out and came inside, leaving a passenger in the car. Glancing over the restaurant in an almost-cop-like fashion, he sat at the counter.

He'd come in behind the captain's back, so Wood continued talking like there wasn't someone new in there. "Do you really think you're ready?"

"I do. The bullet wound is healed, and my knee is much better. I hardly even use the cane anymore. In fact, it was in the cabin when it burned." Their coffee came and Greg took a drink before opening one of the abused packets of sugar and dumping it in. "I want to set up a raid. Say we got some information about a meeting of the gang. Hopefully, they'll take the bait and try to ambush us like the last time."

Wood grimaced. "And get another cop killed? Maybe this time it'll be you."

Greg grinned. "This time we have a secret weapon. Although Adams has already met Kynth. Hopefully it will take him and the other two he had with him a while to get back to town."

"Greg, I don't know what you two are talking about, but stop."

"What's up?" His pulse raced. He held his finger over his mouth in a 'quiet' sign to Wood.

"There's a car parked right beside your booth. A man got out of it and came into the restaurant. Another man is still in it and has some type of long-range listening device."

It was all Greg could do to not get up and go question the man at the counter. Instead, he took Ken's phone out of his pocket and opened the notepad. *Someone is listening to us.* He turned the phone to Wood and tilted his head toward the man at the counter.

Wood handed the phone back and Greg typed. *He's in the car that guy just got out of.*

"Do you recognize him?" he asked Ken.

"It isn't anyone I've seen before. I'm going to try to get his license number." Knowing where he'd left Ken, Greg wasn't surprised at the pause, and figured he was moving carefully over to where he could see the back of the car, which might not have been overly easy with Casey in his arms. *"Here's the number."*

Greg typed in the number as Ken read it to him and then showed it to Wood.

Wood nodded and winked. "You'll be in tomorrow?"

"Yep." Greg grinned. "Rearing to go."

"See you then." Wood got up and left.

Greg waited a few minutes before he got up and hurried out of the restaurant. He walked around behind the café. A hand clasped his arm, and some unseen forces tingled across his skin. He glanced down and realized he could again see Ken and guessed he'd disappeared.

"You were followed."

Greg turned around. The man from the counter dashed around the back of the building carrying a pistol. *"Let's get out of here."* He took Casey and wrapped himself around Ken's back.

Ken morphed and took off. A torrent of dust and dirt swirled in their wake. It was the only indication of their passing.

The man shot toward the spot where Greg had been. It was too little, too late.

"Where to?" Kynth asked with a soft chuckle as they leveled off just over roof height.

"We need to find a place to stay tonight. Let's go get a room."

* * *

Several minutes later, as they landed on the top of a high-priced hotel near the police station, Greg looked around to be sure no one was near and let go of Kynth's back. He hoped they hadn't bothered putting security cameras on the roof. "Stay here; I'll get us a room." He hurried down the stairs to the top floor, then took an elevator to the lobby. His knee didn't need the stress of going all the way down the ten flights of stairs.

The desk clerk looked up from his book. "Welcome, Detective." It was the same clerk who'd been on duty a few months earlier when Greg had helped bust a prostitution ring operating out of the hotel.

 Greg stepped closer to the desk. "Don't suppose you have an empty room for a few days, Ed?"

He glanced at his computer monitor then nodded. "What floor would you like? We've got openings on most of them."

"I have a dog with me and a friend. Something lower might be easier. I'll need to take the dog to the park."

"All I have open on the first floor is a room with one king-sized bed." Ed clicked some keys on the computer. "I have a room on the second floor with two queens. Make it kind of hard for the dog. You'd have to bring him down the stairs or the elevator."

"The king bed will be okay."

Ed raised an eyebrow. "*That* kind of friend?"

Greg grinned and winked. "He's been around for a few weeks now. I've gotten kind of used to him." He signed the forms Ed slid toward him.

Greg took the key to the room and slowly walked to the room. Everyone he passed on his way, Greg studied as covertly as he could, seeing if they were anyone he recognized. He relayed the room number to Ken so they could meet at the door.

When Greg started to close the door, something prevented him, then Casey yipped softly. Greg stepped out of the doorway for a moment as Ken brushed past him. Seconds later, Ken and Casey appeared in the room. Greg finished closing the door and flipped the security lock behind him.

"I think we need to find a place to pick up some clothes and toiletries. The motel furnishes a few things, but probably not the brand I like. Plus I need to replace my cell phone." He strolled over and hugged Ken.

Ken gave him a quick kiss. "We'd probably better find some form of transportation also. I can't be flying us around town. Too much of a chance of radar picking up something strange. If we get too many unexplained blips, the UFO crazies start showing up and we don't need them accidentally getting evidence something is afoot. Not to mention we don't need more people wandering around who might interfere with your investigation."

Greg nodded and went to the hotel phone. He was thankful he'd thought to memorize the captain's burner phone number. "I'll see if the captain has a car we can use."

About half an hour later, Martha Wood pulled up in front of the hotel.

"Hi, Greg." She didn't get out of the car as they hurried out of the lobby toward her. "Don said you need a vehicle. If you'll drive me home, you can use mine."

"Thanks." Greg grinned. "Let's hope it doesn't get blown up or set on fire." He pointed to Ken. "This is Ken."

Her eyes widened. "I've heard about Ken. My boys overheard Don tell me he's a dragon and they want to see him." She sighed. "Honestly, if I didn't trust Bob to tell the truth after all these years of being married to Don, it would've been a lot harder to swallow. But he's not one to make up stuff. I guess our world has a lot of things in it we don't know about."

Ken slid into the back seat. "You're right there. Maybe when this is all over, they can meet me. Don't want to be seen too much around town. It tends to upset folks. It'll be better if we met up in the mountains. Fewer eyes around."

"I can understand that," Martha agreed.

Greg started to get into the car, then paused. "Martha, do you think Casey could stay with the boys for a few more days? I hate to leave him cooped up in the room."

"Oh, I'm sure they won't mind. He can get to know the fake 'Casey' we adopted. Donnie named him Kasey with a K."

"Good." Greg laughed softly. "I'll be right back." He glanced in the back seat. "Now you two don't talk about me too much." Before they could reply, he hurried back into the lobby and down the hall to their room. He was amazed at how easily everyone was taking Ken being a dragon. The kids wanting to see him, that he could understand, but he'd have expected Martha to be a bit worried about it. But Ken was a good guy and with Bob vouching for him, at least the Wood family was accepting. He wished the whole world could be like that, but he doubted that would ever happen.

Chapter Thirteen

THE NEXT morning, Greg walked into the squad room just as the captain was outlining the day's assignments. He looked around and noticed Murphy was missing along with Strader. "Where're Murphy and Strader?"

The captain looked at his clipboard. "Murphy called in sick, and Strader will be late."

Nancy Whitaker walked over to him. "Where's your handsome friend?"

"I left him up the mountain."

"What do you mean, you left me up the mountain?" Ken's mental voice sounded a bit amused.

"Hush." Greg hoped he didn't do anything odd and alert folks that everything wasn't exactly normal around him. *"I don't want anyone to know you're here."*

"Fine. I'm going to snoop while you pretend I'm not here."

"Just don't let anyone run into you while you're invisible."

Before they could say anything more, Greg's new cell phone chirped signaling a text. *Get out of the building; there's a bomb.* As calmly as he could, he walked over to Wood and showed him the phone. Greg wasn't sure where the message was coming from and didn't trust its authenticity. It was more likely a trap of some sort, but they couldn't risk it.

"Everyone out of the building~" Wood whipped his phone out of his pocket and speed-dialed as he gestured for people to head to the doors. "Bomb squad! We just got notice of a bomb in the squad building. Evacuating."

Greg tried to call the number the text came from. "I'm sorry the number you dialed is not a working number." He shook his head at the captain. "Number's no good."

Officers grabbed guns and cell phones. Nancy headed for the lockers.

"No time for lockers, Whitaker!" Wood ordered. "Out of the building now!"

"My purse!" She objected as she fell into hasty step with everyone else in evacuating the building.

"Out!" Captain Wood pointed to the doors. "Your purse can be replaced; you can't." In the distance sirens wailed.

"Ken, are you out of the building?"

"Right behind you, baby."

They hurried out of the building. Greg kept watching everyone, trying to see who was acting like it wasn't a big deal, but in the confusion of getting everyone clear, he couldn't keep track of the people he suspected, and the ones he didn't know. He wondered why his phone had been the one to receive the text, and how they got the number of the new phone. Were they trying to set him up for something?

Officer Strader pulled into the parking lot and got out of his car as the captain and Greg cleared the doors. "What's going on?"

"We got a bomb threat," the captain snapped as his gaze traveled over the people in the parking lot. "I've called the bomb squad. Where have you been?"

"I had a flat, actually two of them." Strader kicked one of his tires. "I just put new tires on last week. Someone stuck a knife through two of them. I had to wait for AAA to come out."

Captain Wood gestured for people to keep moving. "Alright folks, let's set up a one-block perimeter around the building. Make sure everyone got out. Whitaker, go to the office building over there, get them cleared out. I hope that's the bomb squad I hear."

People hurried off as the captain appointed them tasks. Most folks liked it when someone took charge during an emergency. Police officers were used to following his orders.

"Sounds like someone wanted you to be late. Kind of suspicious." Greg looked Strader in the eye even as people hurried around them. "Like they didn't want you here when the bomb went off."

"Are you saying I had something to do with it?" Strader glared at him through squinted lids.

Greg shrugged. "Just saying it sounds strange to me."

The big black van of the bomb squad roared into the parking lot. It parked near the curb and several men piled out. One of them, a man in a uniform as opposed to a heavy protective suit, hurried over to the captain and they had a quick conversation while the men in the suits rushed into the building.

A quiet hush fell over the gathered people as they waited for the bomb squad to search the building. They didn't have any bomb dogs, and Greg couldn't decide if he was happy about that or not. He never liked the idea of dogs risking their lives in the place of humans, but he knew dogs would be better at finding the bombs quickly. The faster they found the device, if there was one, the sooner they could make the area secure. He was also surprised the bomb squad wasn't using their remote-controlled bombots. Then he recalled the captain mentioning how a couple of them had been blown up recently while on the job. Again, they were something that made the job safer for the humans, and Greg wondered if the Black Fins were behind their destruction. There had to be a connection. He didn't believe in coincidence.

A quarter hour later, one of the men in a bomb suit exited the building with a backpack. "Here's your bomb. It was set to detonate at noon."

Wood approached him and glanced at his watch. "Why didn't it go off? Where'd you find it?"

"Looks like whoever put it together didn't connect all the wires the right way. If they had, it would've blown the building and everything for three blocks sky high. It was in the locker of Officer Strader."

"Honest, Captain, that's not mine. I never saw it before." Strader backed away holding his hands up, palms facing the captain before anyone could say anything. "It wasn't there when I left last night."

Greg frowned. "Who has access to your locker but you?"

"I don't lock it at night." Strader shook his head. "There's usually nothing in it but some pictures and stuff. I take my dirty uniform home every night to clean it and bring another clean one in the morning. You can check my car. It's still in the back seat."

"He's telling the truth. His scent isn't on the backpack." Ken announced.

In all the excitement, Greg had almost forgotten Ken was still around. He hoped he hadn't jumped when Ken's voice sounded in his head. *"Oh, you can smell that good?"*

"You'd be amazed at what I can do; you haven't seen half of it." Ken chuckled. It was soft and sexy. "For one thing, yes, I have an excellent sense of smell. I'm extremely good at tracking. I can even follow a scent from the air."

Greg walked close to the captain and whispered, "Ken says he's telling the truth."

"Thought you said he was up the mountain." The captain frowned and his gaze darted around, but he didn't move his head. "He's here now?"

"Yeah." Greg nodded. "I don't want people to know he's here."

"Where is he?"

Greg swiveled his head. "Somewhere around."

The captain turned around quickly. "Who did that?"

"Did what?" But somehow, Greg knew Ken had bumped into the captain or something else to let him know he was there.

Captain Wood leaned close and dropped his voice. "Someone tapped me on the shoulder."

Greg snickered as softly as he could. "Like I said, he's here somewhere."

Wood stomped over to Strader. "I'm sorry. I'm not saying I don't believe you, but until we find out what's going on, I'll have to take your badge and gun."

Strader nodded. "I understand. I'd feel the same way." He removed his gun and badge. "Am I under arrest?"

"Not for now." Wood took the gun and badge. "Just go on home. I'll be in touch."

"Thanks, Captain." Strader hung his head and stumbled toward his car.

For a moment, Greg felt sorry for him, but if someone was willing to set a bomb in the police station, Strader would be safer away from the place.

The man in charge of the bomb squad strolled back over after talking with the men who had put the backpack bomb in a heavy-duty metal drum that Greg recognized as one they used to safely detonate explosives. "That's all we could find."

Captain Wood nodded. "You're sure."

The bomb squad chief returned the nod. "As far as we can see, the building's clear. You might want to have your people go over their personal areas for any signs of anything suspicious. They know the building better than we do."

"Give them ten minutes." Wood turned from the bomb squad and looked at the gathered officers around them. "Okay folks, you heard the man. Their people have done what they could. We got lucky this time. Go in there and comb through your personal areas. If you find anything out of the ordinary, report it immediately, and don't touch it. We've got ten minutes before these guys go on their way."

They hurried back into the building. Everyone was talking softly, trying to figure out what was going on.

Greg tried to pay attention to the conversations but there were just too many of them. *"Ken can you tell if anyone is acting suspicious?*

Talking about things they couldn't know about?" It was a long shot, Ken wasn't familiar with police protocol or lingo, but he might be able to pick up something Greg couldn't.

"Sorry, too many people talking at once. That and it's all I can do to not bump into anyone." His sexy chuckle sounded in Greg's mind. *"I'm good, but that only goes so far."*

Greg couldn't tell exactly where Ken was, and he hoped he was close by. Knowing he was there to watch his back, gave Greg a strange feeling of security he wouldn't have had a few weeks ago. The world was too strange and getting more dangerous by the minute, but Ken was a comforting presence in his life.

Inside, Greg went to his desk and picked up the landline phone. "Lewis, put a trace on this number and get back to me." He read the number from where the earlier text came. He knew it was going to take a few minutes to run the trace, so he started going through his desk, looking for anything odd or out of place, although he wasn't sure what Adams had changed legitimately and what might be suspicious.

He finished up ten minutes later, as his phone rang. "Yeah."

"Williams, this is Lewis. That number is a pre-paid burner phone. Can't trace it."

"That's kind of what I thought." But he'd hoped there might be some clue there, a lead they could follow back to the Black Fins, who had been lying low since Jackson's death, at least in their drug running activities. Either that or the leak in the department was so big it was a full-blown breach that kept the bad guys four or five steps ahead of the cops, even to the point of keeping the street-side thugs quiet about their activities.

"I can tell you it was purchased at the Chevron on Stark St."

A spark of hope flared in Greg. "The one where we fuel up the patrol cars?"

"Yeah. Let me give you the IMEI number. According to the phone company records, it was activated about nine this morning then disconnected right after it sent you the text."

"Thanks, Lewis." He hung up and hurried to the captain's office where the bomb squad commander was just walking out. "I'll be back in a bit, Captain. Might have a lead."

"Do you want back up?" Captain Wood leaned on his desk. "Not like anyone else around here is doing anything."

Greg shook his head. "I've got all the backup I need."

"Wait for me?"

Greg got into the driver's seat of Martha Wood's car and the passenger door opened and closed.

"So we're on a trail." Ken's voice came out of the empty seat.

"Yeah. Hope this leads somewhere. It would be nice to clear Strader quickly. If he is clean, we need him on the force, particularly as we weed out the ones working with the Black Fins."

"Do you have a plan?" There was a soft rustle of cloth rubbing against cloth, like Ken had just crossed his arms.

"Winging it." Greg felt odd talking to thin air. But, it was better than any casual observer possibly noticing Ken sitting there and making him a target, even if Ken had a better chance of surviving a bullet than a human would. Greg didn't want to take the chance he was wrong about that, and have something happen to Ken.

It only took him a couple of minutes to drive the few blocks from the precinct to the gas station. It wasn't really enough time to have much of a conversation, or make a plan. He thought of all the times he and Jackson had been on raids. No plan really lasted past the first couple of seconds of engagement. It had gotten to the point he actually preferred charging in and seeing what was happening when he got there.

Greg did his best to act calm as he walked into the gas station followed by an invisible Ken.

The clerk looked up from his computer. "Hi, Williams. Thought you were in Hawaii."

"Got back yesterday, Doug." Greg walked over to the counter, careful to add a little extra limp to his movement. The soft sound of

Ken's shoes on the cheap linoleum was the only thing that gave away his presence behind Greg.

"I'd have thought you've have more of a tan." Doug rose from the stool behind the counter.

"Too hot to hobble around on one leg. I stayed in the hotel most of the time. There was always someone to watch at the bar." Greg pointed to the computer on the counter. "Do you keep any record of pre-paid cell phones you sell?"

"You mean like who bought them?" Doug shook his head. "Not really. We keep track of when we sell them, but not to who."

"Can you tell me when you sold this number?" Greg showed him the IMEI number of the phone that made the call.

Doug took a minute and looked something up on the computer. He frowned. "Yeah. I sold that one at 8:30 this morning."

"You don't remember who to? Was it Strader?"

"Haven't seen him for a couple of days." Doug frowned.

"Any chance you've got video of them?" Greg hoped there was something Doug could remember, and baring that, maybe he had video proof.

Doug shook his head. "Williams, we were so busy this morning. It was like half the force was in. Carl called in sick and it was all I could do to keep up with everyone. We've got video, but it's set for offsite back up every two hours and then tape over. We'll have to contact the server to get that video pulled. I can get hold of the boss and see about getting it. Might take a few hours. I could send the files over to the station."

Greg nodded and headed for the door. "That would be great. Thanks. I'm going to fill up the car, it's police business. Put it on the department's bill."

"Will do." Doug pushed some buttons on the register. "Have a good day."

"You too."

Greg walked out to the car and placed the nozzle of the pump into the car's tank.

* * *

113

Ken continued to walk around inside the store. With the place being a hub of police activity, he wanted to make sure nothing was up. He stayed near the door. Since there weren't any other people in the place, he had no trouble keeping an eye and ear on Doug.

Doug picked up the phone and dialed. "Yeah. Williams was just in here. Wanted to know who bought that phone this morning…I told him it wasn't Strader, just like you said to…He left. He's filling up his car… Okay."

Ken grinned at the horrified look on Doug's face as he opened the door and went out. He glanced back and caught the man kissing his cross. Softly chuckling, he reported to Greg what he'd overheard. *"Sounds like this operation is even bigger than you thought. Doesn't sound like we can trust what he said about Strader."*

"I agree. We're going to have to be careful who we let in on things. The only people I trust right now are you and the captain."

Although it warmed his heart hearing how Greg trusted him, Ken wasn't sure how he felt about the captain. Sure he was a relative of Bob's, but he'd just met the man and with people out to kill Greg, he was suspicious of everyone. *"Are you sure about the captain?"*

"I have to be." Greg sounded resolved to that as he hung up the gas pump and opened the car door. *"I've known him since I came out of the academy."* Ken slipped in before Greg could, and slid over to the passenger side.

"I'll trust you on this one, but if he's one of the ones trying to kill you, I'm going to eat him." Ken paused at the darkness in his voice. It had been a long time since he'd gotten as possessive of a human as he was of Greg. It felt good, but he wasn't sure how any of the other dragons would feel about him eating the people trying to kill Greg. Most of the stories of dragons eating humans were just that, stories. He didn't ever remember eating human flesh. There was also the question of the other shifters. He had no idea what they were, and what they were getting out of killing Greg. He hadn't even believed shifters really existed until Ken revealed himself. Ken dropped into quiet

contemplation as Greg put the car in gear and headed back to the police station. He was going to stay close and keep Greg safe.

Chapter Fourteen

A BLOCK from the police station, Greg pulled into the library parking lot. "I just thought of something. I'm going to call the captain and let him know I'm going to run a few errands. Plus I'd like to get a couple more things to wear. We didn't get enough last night."

"I'll meet you back at the hotel. Pick up a couple pair of jeans and some shirts for me." Ken's invisible lips touched Greg's and the heat from his body warmed him. The passenger door of the car opened.

"Where are you going?" A flash of fear shot through Greg. He wasn't sure he liked the idea of Ken going off and leaving him. There was too much danger for both of them.

"I thought I'd hang around the police station for a while. Keep an eye on things and watch for Murphy."

"How far does our telepathy thing reach?"

"Probably as far as we need to today. Don't think it would go all the way to the cabin, but within the city should be fine."

"Okay, keep in touch. I'll let the captain know you're around."

"See you later, baby." There was another soft kiss, then the door closed and Ken was gone.

Greg sat there for a second, then pulled out his phone and called the captain. "Hey, Captain," he said before the captain had a chance to finish answering.

"Williams. What have you found out?" The captain sounded impatient.

"Strader didn't buy the burner phone, or so Doug at the store said." Greg wanted to start with the good news first. "He said it was really busy this morning, but he knew it wasn't Strader. He's going to check with his boss about getting us video footage, but it might take a while."

Captain Wood huffed. "And probably a court order. Yeah, that'll be fun. Do you think he was telling the truth?"

For a second, Greg thought about telling him what Ken had heard, then realized that even though they were talking on their burner phones, there might be a chance Jennings had men with enough tech knowledge to listen in if they caught the captain on the phone. "I'm not sure. He seemed calm enough." Let the Fins think they believed Doug.

"Anything else?"

"Not yet. I've got a couple of errands to do. I might be most of the afternoon" He stopped short of letting the captain know Ken was on his way back to the precinct. He hung up and got busy on his errands. He wanted to get done quickly and get back to the hotel and Ken

Greg's first stop was a computer store on the other side of town where he wouldn't be recognized. He picked up a laptop, a couple of USB sticks, and two tablets. He then drove to a coffee shop that had free Wi-Fi and emailed the captain on the secret email.

I think Strader is in on it. He outlined what Ken had overheard. *I'll be in touch.*

* * *

Ken slipped in the door behind a uniformed officer coming in from the patrol car lot, followed him to his work area, and sat on the uncluttered corner of the desk. If there was one thing he didn't know was where to start figuring out which cops were bad. He'd been relying on Greg and the captain to provide his lead. He just hoped he was going to get lucky and a lead would fall into his lap. Over his long life,

117

he often relied on luck to get things to work out. He had a clear view of the officer's computer screen.

The officer opened his email and typed in his password.

Ken watched as he typed a message. He took a pen and paper out of his pocket, wrote the password, and copied the message. *I saw Williams go to the Chevron station. I don't know what he found out.*

The pen slipped out of Ken's hand and hit the floor.

"What was that?" The officer sat up and looked around. He was a lot jumpier than Ken would've expected a police officer to be. "Where'd that pen come from?"

The captain came to the door of his office. "What's going on, Jacobs?"

"That pen just appeared out of nowhere." Jacobs pointed to the floor.

Nancy Whitaker, at the desk next to him, picked up another pen. "Butterfingers me. I was twirling it like I used to twirl my baton and it slipped out of my fingers." She demonstrated twirling the pen, leaned over, and picked up the dropped one. She stood in front of them and held the pen up with a smirk telling Ken she knew he was there.

Following her lead, Ken took it from her hand, and it disappeared.

Nancy winked at the captain.

"Be careful, Whitaker." He frowned, but there was a playful twinkle in his eyes. "You might have hit someone with that. If you have time to play with pens, I have some filing that you can do."

"It just helps me think, Captain." She sat back at her desk and started typing.

Ken followed her, and was thankful she was neat enough she had a good empty spot on the corner of the desk for him to sit and consider his next move. He quickly decided he should let Greg know what had happened.

"Greg?"

"Yeah."

"Where are you?" He hoped Greg had had time to finish his shopping. It hadn't taken him very long to get some information to report.

"I'm in a coffee shop." He took a sip of his latte, the warm, heavy taste of it carried through their link. *"What's up?"*

Ken read off the password and email address. *"One of the beat cops, named Jacobs, just sent an email to this address. See if you can find out who it belongs to."* With the number of people involved in the police corruption, and if they were right and it was tied back to the Black Fins who were some kind of shifter, Ken couldn't understand what a group of shifters would get out of killing Greg. It didn't make any sense. There had to be something big they were all missing. Something like an elephant standing in the room.

"I'm not sure who I can trust to look this up, but I'll see what I can do," Greg replied, then broke their connection.

Ken continued to watch the cops move around the room. He wasn't knowledgeable enough to spot anything that looked like strange behavior. He wished he could talk with Whitaker, or make a connection with her, but he didn't want to do anything that might risk his connection with Greg.

The captain stormed out of his office. "Whitaker, you're with me!"

She grabbed her jacket from the back of her chair and followed him. "Where to, Captain?"

Ken got off the desk and followed them out the door.

"Got a lead on the bomb we need to check out," the captain explained as they hit the cool air beyond the building.

He got into the driver's seat of his patrol car and she climbed into the passenger side.

Ken opened the back passenger-side door and slipped in, causing the car to shift and the two police people in the front seat to turn and look through the metal grating in his direction.

Wood chuckled. "Is that you, Ken?"

"Yep." Ken wondered how anyone ever got comfortable in the back seat of a police car. It was a bit cramped and smelled odd. He couldn't exactly place the stench. "Nice trick with the pen, Whitaker."

"Thanks." She beamed a bit as she turned back to face the front of the car and put on her seat belt. "Where we going, Captain?"

"You'll see." He glanced in the rearview mirror as if trying to see Ken. "Do you know where Williams is?"

"He's at a coffee shop. I'll find out where it is." Ken reached out through their bond to Greg. *"Hey, the captain, Whitaker and I are heading your way. Where are you?"*

Greg chuckled. *"I thought you said you were good at tracking."*

"I am, but I'm hoping you can save me some effort."

"So I'm dating a lazy dragon." Greg chuckled again. *"I'll remember that in the future."* He relayed the address of the coffee house.

"He says he's across the river on 13th Street." He kept his attention divided between Greg and the people in the car with him. *"So we're dating? You're not mad at me anymore?"*

Greg gave a thick mental sigh. *"No. Honestly, I don't think I really was. It's just this whole dragon thing was a bit unexpected and it would've been nice to have it come out a few weeks ago as I was getting to know you as opposed to in the heat of battle. Can you understand that?"*

"I know where that is, Captain." Whitaker pointed toward the Interstate. "It's close to my house. In fact, I stop there often on the way to the precinct."

Wood pulled onto the highway. "Ken, do you think you could show yourself? It's unnerving talking to someone who isn't there; it's like talking to a ghost."

Ken chuckled. "No problem, Captain." He materialized. "I can understand. I just wasn't sure how you'd react. My kind survive by staying secret. There is always a chance someone won't understand. I'm thankful you do."

"Yeah. Me too." The next taste of Greg's latte came through their link. It was a strange overlapping of what Greg was experiencing and the rancid smell in the back of the squad car.

"It also seems like everyone is accepting you. When we get through will all this, I want us to spend some time re-getting to know each other," Greg said. *"Now that I know your big secret, I'd like to fit all the puzzle pieces together to see the complete Ken."*

"Last time this many people found out about me, I was driven out of the area. That's when I came to America. If you want, we can go back up the mountain and spend the winter alone. It's nearly impossible to reach the cabin in the winter." Ken loved the idea of spending the winter with just him and Greg. It would be a nice change of pace, even if it might impact him making the deadline on the books he had due.

* * *

Greg watched the patrol car pull in and park. From Ken, he knew how close they were, but his heart still raced as he watched Ken slip out of the car. The three of them strolled into the shop, ordered coffee, and came to his table.

Ken leaned in and kissed his cheek. "You okay?"

"Better now." Ken's warm lips made his heart skip a beat, but Greg pushed the feeling aside, they had work to do. He handed one of the new tablets to Wood.

"What's this?" Wood looked at the message on it: *We can't be sure we aren't being overheard. Someone could have slipped a small bug into a pocket without you ever knowing it. Whatever you have to say, type on here and we'll exchange tablets to talk.*

"Just a little something I picked up for you." Greg motioned for Whitaker and Wood to share the tablet and scooted closer to Ken so he could watch what he wrote.

The barista brought their orders. "Anything else."

Ken smiled at her. "Not right now."

She went back to the counter.

I haven't had a chance to check out that email address. I'm not sure who to trust to do it: Greg typed

They switched tablets.

Whitaker took the pad and typed: *I have a cousin in IT. I'll contact him.*

Greg typed back: *Don't leave a trail.* He got up, walked to the counter, and came back with a fresh cup of coffee. If he kept drinking at the rate he was going, he wasn't going to be able to sleep for a week.

When he got back to the table, Whitaker was on her phone speaking in a foreign language. It went on for a few minutes, and then she typed: *What's the email address?*

Ken typed it on the tablet, and she returned to the phone. After a couple more minutes, she ended the call.

Ken spoke to her in the language she'd used.

She nodded with a grin.

"Okay." Greg looked at him. "What's going on?"

"I told you I'm from Wales." He smiled. "She was speaking Welsh, or Cymraeg."

Whitaker chuckled. "My great-grandparents were from Wales. All my cousins and I were taught Welsh from a wee age. We've used it a lot of times when we didn't want someone to understand us." She frowned. "It's something none of us has even shared with our spouses. I suppose I should teach my children."

Ken nodded. "It would be good for them to know their heritage."

Wood set his cup on the table. "What did your cousin say?"

"He'll do what he can." Her eyes twinkled with laughter. "He asked if I wanted it 'legal' or 'illegal'."

Greg asked, "And you said?" He didn't like the idea of involving any of Whittaker's relatives, but if it got them the information, hopefully no one else would get hurt.

She glanced sideways at Wood. "Just not to let me know which he used."

The captain nodded, and then typed: *Do you have a plan?*

Greg took the tablet then nodded before he started typing. *I want to set up a dummy raid and let everyone know.*

Where?

Pursing his lips, Greg typed his reply: *I'm thinking the house where I got shot and Jackson was killed. They know we know about that location.* If there was one place on the planet he didn't want to go back to, it was the place Jackson died. He was afraid of the memories it would dreg up. But it also seemed fitting that it might be the same place he could bust the Black Fins for good.

Wood read and nodded. *Do you want SWAT involved?*

I don't know if they can be trusted.

Wood shook his head. *If you think Commissioner Jennings is in on it, I doubt if they can. Who do you want with you?*

Not Whitaker. I think Strader, Ellis, Grant, and Murphy if he shows back up. Greg passed the tablet back to Wood.

Captain Wood frowned. *At least two of those we know are dirty.*

We know they're dirty, and I want them where I can see them.

Glaring at Greg, Whitaker grabbed the tablet. *Why not me? You know you can trust me.*

Yes, I know. Greg knew this was going to be an issue, but he couldn't let her just run off into the line of fire. *But you have a husband and two kids. This is going to be dangerous.*

She fumed as she typed: *I did not join the force to be a pretty 'meter-maid'. My father died in the line of duty. My husband has always supported me, even waited until I was out of the academy to get married. He and the kids understand the danger. Just because I'm a woman shouldn't make a difference. I'm a cop. And a good one.*

Ken put his hand on Greg's arm, sending warm pulses of calm through him. *"I say let her come. She can be invisible on my back. They'll never know she's there."*

"You think so?" Greg worried that even like that, Whitaker would still complain that she was being pushed back to the sidelines. But he'd be willing to let her come that way. He knew she'd be safe with Ken.

"Positive." Ken grinned mischievously. *"I think she'll love riding a flame-throwing dragon into the fray."*

Greg relayed Ken's idea to Wood and Whitaker.

She jumped up, ran around the table, hugged Ken, and spoke in Welsh.

Ken shrugged at Greg. *"Told you she'd like it."*

"It isn't nice to say, 'I told you so.'" Greg started running through raid scenarios in his head, trying to come up with the best one. The one least likely to get anyone killed in the process. He hoped having Kynth along was going to even out the playing field, especially since they still didn't know what kind of shifters the Black Fins were, or how Jennings fit into everything. For all they knew there was a bigger shark out there pulling his strings and everything could still unravel.

"Oh, before I forget,"—Whitaker rummaged in her purse—"Sharon Jackson dropped this off for you." She pulled out a flash drive and handed it to Greg.

Greg took it and immediately plugged it into his tablet.

What is it? Wood asked on his tablet.

A large number of files pulled up on the tablet. Each one had a case name Greg and Jackson had worked on. His breath caught. He'd always known Jackson kept extra files on things they were working on, but had never stopped to ask him about them. Sharon must've found them on their home computer.

He quickly brought up the file on the Black Fins. It was huge. There were photos, videos and more.

"Isn't all this stuff you have seen?" Ken asked through their link.

Greg shook his head. He took the captain's tablet and typed. *Jackson's private records on all our cases. Give me a minute to go through this.*

Captain Wood just nodded in reply.

He started with the photos, there were several folders, some with hundreds of shots. Most of them looked like they were taken outside some of the places they'd raided over the past couple of months. Seeing the pictures, something hit Greg; most of the places they raided were near one of the rivers. If Ken was right and they were some kind of aquatic shifter, that made a lot of sense.

There were series of pictures, like they'd been taken by motion-sensitive camera in rapid succession. One series caught his attention as he scrolled through. A man who looked a lot like Jennings walked from the building they'd raided a week before Jackson was killed. In the set of twenty seven pictures, he headed for the river. There weren't any cars around. He was pulling off clothes as he went, then in the last shot, he was jumping in the river, but his skin looked odd, like it was suddenly sleek and black. Greg stared at it, trying to get a good look and make sure it wasn't just some trick of shadow.

He pushed the tablet with the picture still up at Ken. *"Is that what I think it is?"*

Ken frowned down at it. *"A man shifting into something black as he's diving into the river."* A deep growl escaped Ken. *"This is why they've been trying to kill you, and they killed Jackson. They're trying to protect their secret."*

Whitaker tapped on the table and glared at them. Then made a questioning gesture. "Well?"

Greg took her tablet as Ken turned theirs around so she and the captain could see. *This is what got Jackson killed. He photographed Jennings shifting and diving into the river. Go back a couple of shots and you can see it's Jennings very clearly.* He passed their tablet back and for a moment both tablets were on the other side of the table.

Captain Wood's breath came out in a sharp his. "Son of a bitch."

"You can't use this information," Ken said. *"I'd get in a lot of trouble exposing more shifters. This can't be used as evidence in court. We'll have to find another angle."*

"Don't worry. We will." Greg wondered why Jackson hadn't shown him the photo, then remembered Jackson had been really agitated the night of the raid. Greg had written it off as pre-raid jitters; even veteran cops like Jackson got them. But if he'd been trying to figure out what the picture was and meant, that would explain a lot. He wondered if Jackson had showed it to some else in the department, one of the dirty cops. That could've started the whole ball rolling. Right then and there, everything made sense. He didn't know how, short of

killing him, he was going to make Jennings pay for everything he'd done to both of them.

Ken looked at the files again, and then typed: *Have you noticed all of the cops we think are bad have straight black hair? Not like Native Americans, more like it's slicked back with something. There's also something about their eyes. I can't put my finger on it, but they're strange.*

Greg typed: *Come to think of it, you're right about the hair. I hadn't noticed the eyes.*

Whitaker took the tablet. *I noticed they seldom blink. Murray just seems to stare at me when he talks to me.*

Ken wrote: *That could be a characteristic of their other form.*

Greg tilted his head. *"Kind of like your hair color is the color of you in dragon form?"*

Ken nodded, looking like he'd just revealed a major secret of his people.

Greg felt an inner confidence that he was beginning to understand how shifters worked. He was sure if he had enough time, he'd eventually be able to notice the little nuances that shifters had even when they were in their human forms. He was a good detective, he'd horned his observation skills over the years. Adding shifters to his world was just going to be another thing he'd have to learn to look for.

Chapter Fifteen

AT THE hotel, once they finished making love and he was still feeling the giddy afterglow, Greg ran his fingers over Ken's jaw line and smiled. "I have a few more questions for you."

"Do you think it's safe to talk out loud?" Ken rolled over until he was halfway on top of Greg.

"You may be right. Anyway, dragons are reptiles. Don't they lay eggs? Were you born or hatched?" Greg ran his hands down Ken's back, enjoying the play of the firm muscles there. He always loved feeling an in-shape guy. *"Also, I thought reptiles were cold-blooded, and you're always warm."*

Ken kissed him before answering. *"My parents were in human form when I and my twin sister were conceived. Therefore, my mother was in human form when we were born. As to body temperature, it comes from the fire that is always burning in me."*

It was the most information Greg had gotten out of Ken about his family, but he wanted more. He wanted to know everything, but acknowledged they probably didn't have time to go into it right then and there. *"Are they still alive, and where is your sister?"*

"My father was killed at the Battle of Bosworth Field in the fifteenth century during the War of the Roses." Ken nibbled Greg's ear.

"Which side was he on?" He turned his head to give Ken better access to his neck.

"He was on the side of Richard III against Henry Tudor." Ken accepted the invitation to nuzzle Greg's neck.

"So, even though you're over a thousand years old, you aren't immortal? How was he killed?" Greg wondered if Ken would tell him that, even as close as they were. To reveal something like that was to show a lot of confidence that Greg would never turn on him. That was something Greg couldn't dream of doing in the first place.

"It's hard to kill us in our dragon form, but easy when we're in human form, just like you were able to kill the men at the cabin that day. He was felled by a Tudor archer. The arrow pierced his heart."

"Your mother?" Greg continued to run his hands over Ken's back and wondered if he'd ever get used to the feel. It was magnificent.

"She's still alive in Wales somewhere. She took another mate after my father's death. I don't see her but about every fifty years or so."

"Something bothers me about the first encounter with Hudson at the cabin."

"What?" Ken nibbled on Greg's ear and let his fingers slide down his chest.

"When you and Carter were talking about you eating Hudson. Have you ever eaten a human?"

Ken frowned thoughtfully. *"Not that I know of."*

"How could you eat a human and not know it?"

"Once in the Middle East, I was fed things that I had no idea what I was eating. I don't think any of it was human, but I couldn't swear to it. I know there are a lot of old stories about dragons eating people, but most of them are just tales made up by scared people. Enough talk." Ken rolled over pulling Greg on top of him.

"For now. But don't think this conversation is finished." Greg covered Ken's mouth with his and straddled his legs. They were going to have plenty of time to finish getting all of Ken's story, and being a thousand years old, it was going to be a very long story. Greg was more than happy to take a break and enjoy Ken's centuries of sexual practice.

The Black Fin Case

* * *

The next morning, Greg woke as the sun streamed through the curtains. He was wrapped in Ken's arms and Ken was already awake and watching him.

Without a word, Ken leaned into Greg and kissed him. It was a perfect way to wake up after a long night of stories and love making. Even with the little bit of sleep they'd gotten, Greg wasn't tired. He felt like he was back in his twenties and able to go days on end with just caffeine and sex.

Finally, their kiss broke and Greg rolled away from Ken and swung his legs off the bed. "I don't know about you, but I need a shower and breakfast." He hurried for the bathroom.

Ken followed close behind and buried his face in the back of Greg's neck. "Sounds good to me."

As Ken dressed after their long shower, Greg opened up his email and found a message from Whitaker.

Captain gave me this email address. Show this to Ken.

"Hey, babe, you need to read this." Greg shifted slightly to the side to make it easier for Ken to see his screen. "I think it's in that language you and Whitaker were using yesterday."

Ken looked at the message. "It says the email belongs to Murphy."

Greg grinned a self-satisfied grin. It was nice to know his detective instincts were proving right. "So we were right about him. Call Whitaker and see if he came in this morning. See if she knows what his excuse for yesterday was."

Ken dialed and said a few words in Welsh. "She said he has a bandage on his hand. Said he burned it on a hot pan the night before."

"Tell her we'll be in later." Greg suddenly wondered if Murphy might've been the one making the bomb. Then he remembered how the FBI guy with Hudson had healed so quickly when shot in the knee. Ken had said something shortly after that about quick healing being a shifter gift. If Murphy had a bandage, either the damage had been a lot, he wasn't a shifter, or the bandage was a fake. But that complicated the idea that all the Black Fins were shifters.

Ken repeated the message and then asked Greg, "Breakfast?"

129

Greg shrugged. They hadn't taken time to eat yet. He was hungry. "Breakfast." He hoped they could get somewhere they could talk without having to use any trickery. It was getting old fast.

"Do you care where?" Ken asked. After Greg shook his head, Ken told Whitaker where they were going. They were out the door a couple minutes later.

As they sat in the Burger King close to the precinct, Wood and Whitaker joined them.

"Fancy seeing you two here." Whitaker set her tray on the table and slid into the booth next to Ken.

Wood placed a cup of coffee on the table and handed a tablet to Greg.

I told the squad this morning that we had information of a meeting at the Black Fin house tonight and ordered them to be ready to strike at 8 o'clock.

"You two know if you keep leaving together like this, the office gossips are going to have you having an affair." Greg typed back: *Do you want me to come in today?*

Captain Wood choked slightly on his breakfast sandwich as he accepted the tablet back. He glanced at Whitaker and quickly responded to Greg's message on the tablet: *Not until this evening. Everyone else will think I've sent Whitaker home at the usual time. She's going to raise a fuss like she did yesterday. You can figure out where she and Ken can meet up.*

Whitaker grinned at the captain. "You know, if we are being watched, maybe we should put on a bit of a show for them. Give them fodder for their gossip. It might also help us ferret out some more bad guys."

"No." The captain frowned at her and finished off his coffee. "We better get back before the loose lips start flapping."

"Okay." Whitaker finished off her breakfast, then followed him out the door, taking the opportunity to pinch his butt when he stopped to put his garbage in the can.

He turned and glared at her.

Greg choked back a guffaw as he got up to refill his and Ken's coffee. Whitaker seemed to be having too much fun with things, but he trusted her impeccably. He remember how he'd trusted Hudson too. In his years as a cop, he'd never worried about the other officers on the force. They'd always been part of a family, he didn't like the idea he was having to question everyone and everything that happened around him. He remembered one of his instructors at the academy telling him that when he had to start watching his back every second, it might be time to find a new job. Greg loved being a cop, but the idea of living in a small cabin by a mountain lake while making his living doing woodwork was gaining momentum in his brain. When everything was said and done, he wanted to talk to Ken about it.

Ken finished off his refilled coffee and set the cup down with a sharp clap on the table. *"If I'm going to carry Whitaker tonight, I need to go back to my cabin for a few minutes. Will you try to stay out of trouble while I'm gone?"*

The sound of the cup and Ken's thoughts, brought Greg out of his introspection. He looked at him open-mouthed. *"Stay out of trouble? What do you mean?"*

Ken tilted his head a glared at him.

"Okay. I think I'll drive over to the captain's house and check on Casey while you're gone. How long will that be?"

"I'll only need a few minutes at the cabin, so I shouldn't be gone much over a couple of hours. It's been a century or two since I've carried a lady on my back."

"Whitaker isn't a lady; she's a cop."

"She's still a female. They do have different anatomy from males. I'll be at the hotel when you get back."

Ken left and Greg watched as he went behind a building next door. Soon a faint, fuzzy shadow passed overhead. *"See you soon."* It felt odd saying goodbye to someone he couldn't actually see. But Greg couldn't deny there was something about Ken he was accepting as part of his life. It was strange and different, but it felt good. Ken kept him warm in several ways, and he wasn't about to do anything that was going to disrupt that. He wanted to find out where it was going to lead.

"Be careful."

The caring that came through the thought was clear and brought a wide smile to Greg as he started the car. He couldn't remember the last time he felt cared for the way he did when Ken was around. On second thought, it was when his grandmother was still alive.

* * *

Two hours later, a knock sounded on the door of the motel room, and Greg opened it. He looked around and saw no one.

"You can close the door, babe. I'm in."

Greg jumped slightly, then spotted Ken sitting on the bed with the leather harness lying next to him. A padded seat had been added to the harness. Having a boyfriend who could become invisible might take more getting used to than one who could become a dragon. Would he ever be able to know he was alone in a room again?

"You scared me." He walked over and kissed him.

Ken grinned. *"Sorry. I didn't want to be seen."*

Greg straddled Ken's legs and sat on his lap. *"You seem to be good at not being seen. Let's hope you and Whitaker can keep it up tonight."*

Ken kissed his nose, and then lowered his lips to Greg's. *"How long before we meet Wood, and where am I supposed to meet Whitaker?"*

"We have a couple of hours." Greg realized Ken must not have been reading the tablet as they got the details ironed out before leaving Burger King. *"I'm going to the precinct, and Whitaker is coming here after she fusses at the captain for not letting her go on the raid."*

"A couple of hours." Ken nuzzled along Greg's chin. *"What should we do for a couple of hours?"*

Greg pushed the harness out of the way and shoved Ken down on the bed. He ran his hands under his shirt. *"I can think of something."*

The Black Fin Case

He had never spent the time before a raid having sex. It made having Ken around all the more exciting.

Chapter Sixteen

AS GREG reached the door of the squad room, the knob was pulled out of his hand by an irate Whitaker.

"Just wait, Captain!" she shouted over her shoulder. "I'm going to file a discrimination charge. Just because I'm a woman. I'm a better cop than half of the men in this precinct. And don't say it's because I have a family. Most of the men have families also." She pushed against Greg's chest throwing him off balance. "Get out of my way, you…you…you *man*."

Greg threw his hands up as if surrendering, stepped back, and watched as she stormed out the front door of the precinct. He admired her acting ability. In his mind's eye, he could see her carrying her performance all the way down the steps and not stopping until she was in her car. If he hadn't known she was faking, he'd have believed it. The sound of tires squealing carried through the main door as someone opened it, heading out in her wake.

Greg continued into the squad room, ran his finger across his forehead, and shook it as if he were shaking sweat off. "Whew, what was that all about, Captain?"

"I was just getting ready to call you." The captain followed him. "I got word that the Black Fins are meeting tonight in that house where you and Jackson were ambushed. We're going to hit it in a couple of hours."

Greg sat on the corner of his old desk.

"Whitaker got upset when I told her I didn't want her there."

Greg continued to act surprised. "Do you think she'll really file a discrimination report?"

"Who knows?" Wood picked up a pencil from the desk. "She may cool off." He grinned. "She takes after her old man, though. He used to blow up at the drop of a hat, and then cool down and see reason."

"Do you think they might ambush us again, Captain?" Strader asked, not looking overly concerned. Greg was a little surprised to see him back at his desk, but it didn't take long to reinstate someone, and if he wanted to maintain his cover in the department, he couldn't stay out after he'd been cleared. They were still waiting for the tapes from the gas station to see who had actually bought the phone, even if it looked more and more like Strader had done that too.

"I don't know Strader. We know Hudson was a leak and it looks like Adams might be working with them also. I want you, Murphy, Williams, Jones, Ellis, Grant, and Billings. Murphy, you're with Billings, come in from the east to the south end of the alley; Strader with Grant from the west to the north end. Williams with Jones from the south, and Ellis and I from the north. Park at least a block away and walk in. When we get to the alley, Murphy guard the south entrance to the alley and Billings join Williams and Jones. Strader take the north entrance, and Grant join me and Ellis. We're not going to lock down the area like we normally do. Be careful of civilians."

* * *

Ken opened the door to Whitaker's knock. He'd heard her footsteps coming down the hall and caught a whiff of her perfume. It was light and floral.

She smiled as he stepped aside to let her in. "Hi, handsome. I'm ready for my dragon ride."

Ken projected his thoughts into her head. *"Careful what you say. This place may be bugged."*

Her eyes widened. "How did I hear you?"

"It's called telepathy. Just think what you want to say to me or speak in Welsh." He didn't bother telling her he hoped communicating with her didn't interrupt his link with Greg. Ken hadn't had cause to try linking to two people at the same time in many years, and the last time one of the people had been another dragon which made things a lot easier.

"Like this?" There was a little bit of mirth in her mental voice. *"We don't want to use Welsh and let them in on our secret?"*

"You got it! We have some time yet. Greg's going to tell me when they head out." He indicated a table where a pizza and some sodas sat. He'd taken a chance and just got basic pepperoni pizza and Coke in the hopes she'd like it. Greg had mentioned she'd probably come over without stopping for food, and he felt it was a good idea to give her some nourishment before the bullets started flying. *"Have something to eat. You look hungry."*

"Hope I don't get air sick." She sat in a chair and picked up a slice of pizza.

"You hope?" He grinned. *"I'm the one who should be hoping. I wouldn't want half-digested pizza all over my back."*

"I'll try not to." She giggled. *"You should have seen the look on Greg's face when I pushed him out of the way a few minutes ago."*

"Good show?" Ken sat on the other side of the table and poured himself a cup of soda.

She swallowed. *"I wish I had a video of it."*

Greg's thoughts came into Ken's mind. *"She should win an Oscar for her performance."*

"You're picking us up?"

"Reading you loud and clear; Whitaker too."

"Three-way connection isn't uncommon. I've had it happen a couple of times, but it's usually with two dragons and one human."

"This is fun." Whitaker inserted.

* * *

As Whitaker finished off the pizza, Greg's voice sounded in Ken's head, *"Are you two ready?"*

"Almost." He wasn't going to fail Greg when the chips were down.

"We're leaving the precinct. See you in the alley."

"Be careful." Ken carried his cup to the garbage can and dropped it in.

Greg chuckled softly and for a second it felt like he kissed Ken. *"You too."*

"Okay, Whitaker." Ken picked up the harness of the bed. The leather wasn't very worn, he had fewer riders than he did people he bothered communicating mind to mind with. Even though he'd had the harness created several hundred years earlier, it had only been used a few times. Ken always kept it oiled and in good shape, just in case the need arose for him to have a passenger. *"Time to go."*

"Be right back." She hurried into the bathroom.

While she was gone, Ken donned the harness. It was overly loose on his human form, but would fit perfectly in his dragon form. The pad rested on his hips. He was thankful dragons didn't tend to do much changing once they reached their adult size, otherwise he might've had to get the harness resized, and he wasn't sure a modern saddle maker would be up for the task of creating something for a dragon. There were just too many little tricks of most of the trades that had been lost over time, or replaced by technology, and his harness wasn't something he wanted to risk to lack of knowledge or creativity.

"I think I'm ready." Whitaker came back into the room wiping her hands down her pant leg.

"Have you ever ridden a horse?"

She paused and studied the leather draping him. *"Years ago when I was a kid."*

"See these straps." He fingered the ones that ended in loops.

"The ones that look like stirrups? Yeah."

"Once I morph, put your feet into them and hold on to the strap in front of you. Like I told Greg, it's been a couple of centuries since I carried a lady. Then the woman wore a long heavy skirt and insisted on riding side saddle with her leg hooked over one of my ridges."

She grinned. *"No reins?"*

"I'll do the steering." He lowered his head and glared at her before he went invisible. *"We need to get to the roof. I can't fit in the elevator or the halls in my dragon form."*

They hurried along, Ken was thankful the harness didn't have much in the way of buckles to jingle as they went along. It was late enough; they didn't pass many people in the hall. The elevator was empty when it arrived, and Whitaker hit the button for the top floor. They rode up in silence. Ken kept a mental ear out for Greg. When they reached the stairwell, there wasn't anything he could do to keep the sounds of their passage quiet there, but they only had to go up one flight to get to the roof. A brisk wind met them as they opened the door, and it smelled like snow was coming.

In the shadows of the rooftop, Ken dropped his invisibility for a moment to make it easier for Whitaker. *"Now, get on my back 'piggy-back' style and put your legs around my waist."*

She did as he said.

Ken picked up a small gasoline can he'd put up there earlier in anticipation for their flight. It had been easier to get it up there when he hadn't had the harness on.

"What's that for?"

"You'll see later." He resumed invisibility, morphed, and launched himself into the night sky.

Whitaker let out a soft squeal that sounded like a mix of delight and fear. She squeezed her legs tight around his back and held the ridge in front of her as Ken pumped his wings and carried them off to meet up with Greg. He hoped they weren't too late and the Black Fins wouldn't ambush Greg and the captain before they reached the house.

* * *

A feeling of déjà vu settled over Greg as he made his way toward the door of the house. Although the stench wasn't as strong because the temperature wasn't as hot, it still caused him to gag. *"Are you here, Ken?"*

"Looking right at you, baby."

"How's Whitaker?"

Ken's deep chuckle reverberated in Greg's mind. *"Mad because I wouldn't give her reins to steer with."*

"Just like a man. He has to be in control." Whitaker lightly slapped Kynth's neck.

Greg wanted to look around and see if he could spot anything that might tell him where Ken was, but he stayed focused on the door in front of him. *"Where are you exactly?"*

"Right on top of the house." He paused. *"Heads up; here they come."*

Greg waved to Wood on the other side of the door. *"Whitaker the two at the ends of the alley are yours. Try not to kill them."*

"Got it." Whitaker's chuckle sounded in his mind.

The black SUV screeched around the corner and, ignoring Murphy, headed for the line of men approaching the door.

Out of nowhere, an open can of gasoline landed in front of the van followed by two bursts of flames which ignited the gas causing it to flare up as high as the top of the vehicle.

The driver slammed on the brakes and came to an abrupt stop; Adams, Jacobs, and three other men piled out, guns blazing and were met with a wall of riot shields.

* * *

Kynth materialized and swooped down toward Strader.

"Hi-ho, Silver, away!" Whitaker yelled as she aimed and fired. Strader went down.

"Hang on Whitaker; it's about to get bumpy." Kynth switched directions in mid-air and Whitaker took out Murphy. He again turned. Jacobs had an assault rifle aimed at Greg. Kynth let out a loud roar and dived for him. *"Oh, no, you don't. I've got this one."*

He swooped and picked the screaming man up with his front feet. *"Meet you back at the precinct."* He called to Greg as he took off flying as hard as he could. The man was a lot heavier than he expected.

Whitaker looked down over Kynth's shoulder. *"What are we going to do with him?"*

139

"Thought maybe a bar-b-que."

"I think he'll be too tough and gamey," she said out loud.

Jacobs shuddered and there was a tingling in Kynth's foot. He recognized a shifter trying to change. He squeezed tight with one foot, then thumped his captive with the other. Jacobs went limp and became lighter. Kynth knew then the man's other form was larger than human.

Kynth became invisible and flew toward the precinct. He landed in the parking lot, and Whitaker dismounted.

"Where are you taking him?"

"Someplace where I can question him after he wakes up. Tell Greg I'll talk to him later."

* * *

In the interrogation room, Greg and Wood sat across a table from Adams.

"So, three dead; Strader and Murphy in the hospital; and we don't know where Kynth took Jacobs." The captain leaned across the table and glared at Adams. "Talk!"

"I've got nothing to say." Adams glared. "I'll wait for my lawyer."

Whitaker walked into the room.

Greg turned toward her. "Pretty good job, Whitaker." He winked at her. "You still going to file that discrimination suit?"

Her face broke into a wide grin. "I may reconsider. After all, it isn't every day a girl gets to ride a dragon into battle. It was fun."

"What'd you do with Jacobs?" Wood asked.

"I don't know where Kynth took him." She shrugged. "He dropped me off here and took off again muttering something about a bar-b-que and tasting like chicken."

Adams eyes opened wide and he gulped. "Do you think he'll really eat him?"

"I don't know," Greg said. "He told me most dragons prefer virgins, and it's doubtful any of you guys are." He looked at the captain. "You know we could lose the paperwork on these guys and Kynth wouldn't have to eat for months."

Wood pursed his lips and nodded.

Adams jumped out of his chair. "You can't do that!"

* * *

Kynth flew east out of Portland toward Mt. Hood. He reached his lair, landed, carried a still unconscious Jacobs inside, and laid him on a bed of straw. He materialized, morphed into human, and checked him for weapons. He then set about building a fire under a large spit.

Jacobs jerked awake. "Where am I?"

"In my home."

"You." Jacobs back peddled until he flattened against the rocks behind him. "You're the dragon."

Ken simply grinned.

"What are you going to do with me?"

Ken shrugged. "That kind of depends on you."

Jacobs looked at him sideways. "What do you mean?"

"I was thinking bar-b-que, but I don't have any sauce. I guess it'll just have to be plain roasted."

A look of fear crossed his face. "You can't." He started to shift again, then something stopped him. He stayed human.

"Oh, I could. But maybe if you co-operate, I might be persuaded to change my mind."

"What do I have to do?"

"Talk. Who shot Carter?"

"Adams did. He shot him with Carter's own gun."

Ken nodded. "I thought as much." He walked over and stirred the fire. "But we know Adams isn't in charge, he's just muscle. How about some names? Is Jennings the head guy?"

Sweat glistened on Jacobs' face. "You promise not to eat me?"

"Keep talking." Ken walked away from the fire and nodded. He began to think this was too easy.

"Yes, Jennings is our alpha. Adams is his beta. Jennings has contacts in Columbia, and we bring the drugs in from boats that come up the coast and into Tillamook Bay. But you can't stop him. We've got people everywhere."

Ken cocked an eyebrow at the man. "What are you?"

141

"You're a dragon, can't you tell?" The man suddenly sounded cocky. "You're the one who's invaded our land. We never had dragons in North America before the Europeans showed up."

"Yes, I'd heard none of our kind were native to this land. But you aren't a dragon; that much I know." Ken didn't want to take time for a history lesson from his captive. He wanted answers. He was well aware there were some shifters who could tell what other shifters were as soon as they came in contact. He wasn't sure if dragons had ever had that particular gift or not, and he didn't really care. The few times he'd met other shifters, he'd always been polite and asked what they were.

"Then maybe I better just keep quiet about what I am," Jacobs said with a sneer. "I'd always heard that dragons were something to be feared. But you're not that frightening now that you're not going to eat me."

Ken chuckled. "I can always change my mind."

"Yeah, right." Jacobs crossed his arms and glared. "The other thing I've always heard is that dragons, more than any other shifter, keep their word. You told me you weren't going to eat me."

"So I won't. But that doesn't mean I won't kill you and leave you for the ravens." Ken launched himself across the cave at Jacobs, shifting as he did. He buried his claws in the rock on either side of him. "So tell me, or show me what you are!"

Jacobs' skin darkened with a white strip running across his face and down his neck. He whistled and slipped out of Kynth's claws. He hit the floor of the cave with a flop and continued shifting.

Kynth jumped back and watched as Jacobs' clothes fell away and his body became long and heavy, not at all designed to be on land. He was a creature of the sea, made for hunting in packs, and capable of taking on prey many times his own size. He'd heard rumors of them, and that they controlled the shifter populations along the coast, he just hadn't run into any of them.

The Black Fin Case

He straddled the orca's back, pinning its flippers to the ground with his talons. "Change back." He hissed as he leaned next to the thing's head.

The orca shifter snapped at him.

Kynth shot a long stream of fire into his fire pit. The flames already there blazed brightly and the temperature in the cave shot up. He knew it wouldn't take long to dry out the whale and if orca shifters were like their oneform cousins, it couldn't survive long without water unless it reverted to human form.

The shift started again and Kynth reared back, releasing the thing's flippers. He shifted back as well, meeting it man to man.

"All right. You've got some more questions to answer." Ken glared and did his best to make sure the other shifter didn't forget how dangerous he was.

A naked Jacobs rubbed his hands, where Kynth's talons had left marks even after he had shifted back to human. "What? You're really going to kill me, aren't you?"

"That's a distinct possibility." Ken reached out to the flames in the fire pit and called a ball of fire to his hands. "When is the next time drugs are coming into town?"

The man laughed. "You don't have time to stop it. It's tonight. Probably happening right now. Unless this cave of yours is on the coast, you'll never reach there in time, and Jennings will probably change up the plans now. He doesn't trust anyone. He'll assume I talked and might even change cities and start up somewhere new, like Vancouver."

Ken wanted to fly out at that moment, but he needed a little more information. One important piece of the puzzle was still missing.

"Why have you been trying to kill officer Williams?"

"That human? He was getting too close. His partner was about to discover what we are. We couldn't let that happen."

"Thanks." Ken hit the man hard. Harder than he would've hit a human, but since he knew the orca shifter could handle it, he didn't hold back.

The man's head jerked hard and he crumpled to the cave floor.

143

Ken morphed and took off as fast as he could, leaving Jacobs unconscious on the floor of the cave. The cave was miles from unfrozen water. The man wouldn't get far in the cold weather without any clothes. He had to let Greg know what was going on, and they had to catch Jennings in the act to stop him for good.

* * *

"They're what?" Captain Wood's mouth dropped open and he stared at Greg after he'd relayed the information Kynth had told him via their link.

"Orca shifters, killer whales." Greg shook his head. Then he recalled the black sickle-shaped fins he'd spotted in the lake when Kynth had flown him to town. "The Black Fins are orca shifters."

The tech guys had just gone over Captain Wood's office again and found three new bugs, two on the desk and one under a plaque near the door. They felt safe talking in the office.

"Regardless of what they are, how are we going to get to Tillamook Bay tonight?" Whitaker asked. "Jacobs is right, if we don't stop them tonight, Jennings will realize how much we know and run. It's now or never."

The captain picked up the phone. "If we're lucky, they'll be busy getting their drugs in and won't stop to realize we're onto them." He dialed a number. "This is Captain Wood. Is the police chopper available?" He paused. "Good. I want it on my precinct roof in ten minutes."

He hung up. "Whitaker. Do I remember one of our guys having contacts in the coast guard?"

She looked thoughtful then nodded. "Ellis. I think his brother-in-law is one of theirs."

"You've got ten minutes. Have him make the connection to get us a cruiser out to the bay. They've got choppers too."

Whitaker dashed out of the office and started shouting for Ellis as soon as she was in the squad room.

Greg shook his head. "If we tell them that whales are running drugs they're going to laugh themselves silly. We need a better plan."

"We don't have time." Captain Wood pulled his service revolver from his desk and slipped it into his shoulder holster. "We've got to move. Trying to explain where Jennings disappeared to if we don't will be enough of a mess."

"And if we don't stop them, it'll be an even bigger mess," Greg said. "Sounds like some kind of race war, or species war brewing. We've got to stop that, or we'll have more dead than just a couple of cops." As the words left his mouth, a chill went through him. He couldn't believe he sounded so casual about Jackson's death. It wasn't right, but if Ken was right and the orca shifters were mad about a land dispute, the whole drug running thing could just be something to destabilize the humans in the area and give them a chance to retake their ancestral home. Wars had been started for a whole lot less.

They filed out of the office, heading for the stairs that would take them up to the helipad on the roof.

"Wait for us!" Whitaker shouted as she and Ellis hurried over.

Ellis had a cell phone to his head. Greg looked at him and wondered if he could trust him. He knew Ellis's family were multigenerational cops. To his knowledge there'd never been a bad one in the bunch. He just hoped that was still the case.

"Chuck says they've got the ships on their radar. They'll be closing in before we can get there." Ellis slipped the phone back in his pocket. "Thanks for including me in on this one, Captain. These guys owe us big time for what happened to Jackson."

"Right." Captain Wood said. "They owe us for a lot of things." They all hurried up the stairs and to the helicopter they could hear above them.

"We're taking to the air," Greg called to Kynth as he got buckled in. *"The Coast Guard is on their way too."*

"I can see a helicopter lifting off from the precinct roof." Kynth sounded tired. *"I'll follow you."*

"Good." Inwardly Greg smiled. Having Kynth not far away made him feel better, and he just hoped they'd be in time to cut Jennings off

at the pass, red handed, or flippered, or however one referred to catching an orca shifter in the act.

* * *

"Ellis, I hope we can trust your brother-in-law," Greg said into the microphone as the helicopter swooped down toward the shore.

"He's married to my sister. With all of the law enforcement in our family, he'd be crazy to be dirty." Ellis grinned. "In addition to myself, I have three brothers and a father on OHPD, and we're all bigger than he is." His face assumed a more serious look. "Chuck said they'd been trying to catch this group for over a year now. Maybe tonight's the night."

The sound of helicopters filled the air, and lights flashed from a ship in the bay. There were several men on the shore and at least two large dorsal fins in the water.

"I've got the shifters!" Kynth shouted in Greg's mind.

"Careful!" Greg replied. He felt helpless in the helicopter. "We need to get down there!"

"I'm working on it!" the pilot replied. "With the Coast Guard birds in the air, we're getting kind of crowded around here."

Greg stayed quiet. Getting upset and pushy wasn't going to help the situation. He just wanted to be on the ground, lending a hand, even as automatic weapons fire erupted below them. He also hoped Kynth was able to dodge the helicopters since they couldn't see him.

One of the Coast Guard choppers got hit and flames came out of its tail. It fell toward the ground as the other chopper lay down a line of gunfire, kicking up plumes of sand in the lights from the Coast Guard cutter just off shore. Greg hoped Kynth was okay. He searched the dark waters below him for signs of either Kynth or the orcas. With the one chopper down, the light was cut back.

"Hang on!" their pilot shouted into the head sets. It came through louder than any of Kynth's thoughts ever had. "We're going in."

Sand flew in all directions as the helicopter landed on the beach. Greg pulled out his gun, suddenly wishing he'd grabbed something more than just his service revolver. He put his hand over his mouth and nose and jumped out of the helicopter. His leg complained, but he ignored it as he took off running in the direction of the two large panel vans pulled near the surf.

Bullets flew around him. Greg ran as low as he could. Since he had a limited number of bullets, he chose targets carefully. His first round took out a tire on the van closest to him. He stopped running for a moment to get a steady shot on one of the bad guys shooting at the helicopters. He dropped him with a single shot to the head. Silently, he hoped the bullet went to his brain. If the man was a shifter, he wouldn't be able to repair that damage.

Bullets hit the sand near him. Greg dropped to the ground.

"Stay down, Williams!" Captain Wood shouted from above him. "I've got this one!"

The captain's gun barked twice and the bullets stopped flying toward Greg. He got to his feet. "Thanks, Captain."

"No problem. Don't want to have another funeral any time soon."

"Damn!" Ellis shouted.

"Ellis, keep low!" Whitaker screamed.

More gun fire erupted.

"Take that you sorry hung son of a bitch!" Whitaker yelled as another bad guy hit the dirt.

"They're trying to escape!" Kynth shouted through his link with Greg.

"What can we do?" Greg wanted to go running into the surf and start shooting whales, but he couldn't see them real well in the darkness.

"This might work, it might not. I've never tried it before." Suddenly, flames erupted on the water. *"We're lucky dragon fire doesn't go out as easily as regular fire."*

Two screaming orcas leapt out of the water. One more went straight up, like it was trying to get to Kynth where he was a strange blur against the starry sky. The source of the flames was the only point that was for sure him.

The flames cut out and Kynth grabbed the whale before it could re-enter the water. He flickered in and out, like it was almost too much strain to keep his invisibility going while he was trying to carry the weight of the whale. He stopped his invisibility completely and managed to get the whale over the beach and dropped it.

"Come on, Captain!" Greg surged to his feet and ran toward the whale as it started bucking on the sand, obviously trying to get back to the water.

Greg and the captain approached cautiously. Greg was thankful there wasn't any further gunfire from the men on shore. He hoped Whitaker and Ellis had stopped them all. He hadn't heard either of the trucks leave. That was a good thing.

"Stop right there!" Greg shouted at the orca as he leveled his pistol at the thing's eye. "I'm a crack shot. I don't think you can survive a bullet to the brain."

"Make that two bullets!" Captain Wood added from the other side of the thing's head.

"Shift!" Greg ordered. "If you don't change, there'll be a whale corpse here on the beach for the seagulls to pick clean in the morning."

Another whale hit the beach just past the captain. This one shifted quickly and rolled on the sand in obvious pain.

Greg grew tired of waiting for the one he had his gun trained on to do something. He shot it in the flank. It squealed. "The next one goes in your eye."

The orca blurred and moments later, Jennings lay naked on the sand. He rolled up and clutched his knee. "Damn it, Williams! You shot me in the knee."

"Stay right there, Jennings!" Captain Wood shouted. "You're under arrest!"

Greg stared at the commissioner. He hadn't really believed it until that moment. He'd always hoped there was going to be another answer, but he couldn't deny the evidence in front of his face. The corruption in the department had started at the head and worked its way down.

"You don't have jurisdiction here!" Jennings ranted. "You can't arrest me."

"But I can." One of the men from the coast guard chopper that had gone down rushed over with his handcuffs out. "Commissioner Edgar Jennings, you've got the right to remain silent..."

Greg blocked out the sound of Jennings getting his rights read to him as he was handcuffed. Lights were appearing on the road leading down to the beach. They were flashing red and blue, the local authorities had finally arrived.

Then strong arms enfolded him from behind. "I think we're done here," Ken whispered in Greg's ear.

Greg turned in his embrace and kissed him. "I think we are. Nothing left now but the paperwork."

Ken frowned at him. "Can't we leave that to everyone else? It's not even your jurisdiction."

"Nope. I owe it to Jackson to see this through. Once Jennings is behind bars, I'll feel better about the whole thing." He felt a certain happiness that he'd wounded Jennings in much the same way he'd been wounded by Jennings' goons, but it wasn't going to bring Jackson back. His partner was gone, but he knew Jackson wouldn't want him to kill Jennings out of revenge. Justice had been more Jackson's way.

* * *

Two hours later, everyone sat in the Coast Guard station in Garibaldi and recapped the night's events. Greg was tired enough he could've done without it, but he understood how these things worked and bore with it.

"That load of cocaine should top out at over twenty-five million dollars," Ellis said. "Hopefully we put a crimp in things."

"If not, this is bigger than one pod of orca shifters," Greg said as he leaned back in the wooden chair that creaked under his weight.

Ken took a sip from a cup of coffee and spit it back into the cup. "I thought the coffee at the precinct was bad."

Whitaker laughed. "I've never tasted good cop coffee. It's only there to keep us going."

"Right," said the captain. "I'm going to issue an order to the gang unit to make sure nobody tries to fill the void the Black Fins are going to leave. I just want to know how we're going to deal with shifters on top of everything else."

"Hopefully the shifters will deal with themselves." Ken settled into the chair next to Greg. "We normally do a pretty good job at flying under the human radar. I'm just hoping we can minimize my involvement in all this, officially anyway. I know there were probably more dragon sightings in Portland the past couple days than there have been in years, even if it was just shadows."

The captain nodded. "I'll see what I can do. The other problem about any of this being official is going to be explaining why a civilian was helping with a major drug bust."

Ellis's brother-in-law appeared and leaned against the doorframe. "No worries on that. We've got enough confusion with you all from Portland showing up to help. We're not going to worry about one little myth come to life lending a wing. This is the biggest bust we've had in a long time. By the time the excitement wears off, they won't even remember you were here, unless Jennings gets talkative."

"Thanks." Ken said. "Jennings isn't going to be a problem. I've gone in and made a few adjustments in his brain. He's so upset by the bust and all the drugs he's been taking he won't be making much sense for a while." He yawned. "I'm about ready to head back to my little place in the mountains and stay there for the winter. I think I'll make a similar adjustment to Jacobs and drop him off at the precinct before we call this all done. But I definitely need some down time."

Greg couldn't think of anything he'd rather do. "Me too."

Chapter Seventeen

THE SUN was rising as Greg turned into the parking lot of the Burger King.

"Where are you going?" Ken asked.

"After all that crappy coffee we've been drinking, I thought some breakfast and decent coffee might help me sleep." Greg parked the car and turned it off.

"Coffee doesn't help you sleep." Ken got out and the two of them walked to the door.

"The way I feel now, I don't think anything could keep me awake, and I'm hungry." Greg resisted the yawn that tried to escape him. He felt like a walking dead man, even if the danger to him was past. He wanted nothing more than to head back to the hotel, curl up with Ken and get some sleep, but knew if he didn't eat something first, he'd feel worse when he woke up.

They got their orders and sat across from each other at a small two-top table.

Ken swallowed a bite of his croissant sandwich. "So what are you going to do now that the case is closed? You'll need to look for a house; you can't keep living in a hotel. It wouldn't be fair to Casey."

Greg hesitated. He wasn't sure how Ken was going to react to what he planned. "I'm thinking about quitting the force." He'd been giving it a lot of thought and he needed a change. He didn't want to keep doing what he'd been doing for years. It just seemed like he was always going to be fighting a losing battle against the bad guys. Sure, they'd taken down the Black Fins, but who was going to rise up in their place? He wanted his own life, one where he wasn't going to be afraid like he had been since Jackson was killed. No one should have to live in fear.

"Why?" Ken set his sandwich back on its wrapper. "I thought you loved being a cop."

"I did until Carter and Jackson were killed. Carter's death was just so senseless." He sipped his coffee. "Also, the thought of so much corruption just soured me. To think I worked with those guys and trusted them."

Ken touched Greg's arm. "What will you do?"

"I don't know." Greg ran his fingers around the top of his coffee cup. "Like you said, I don't have anywhere to live. I do have the insurance money from the house fire. I could live on that for a while." He wadded up the paper from his sandwich.

Ken tilted his head. "You don't think you should put it into another house?"

Greg pursed his lips and shook his head. "I'm not sure. I liked living in the cabin away from the city the past few weeks; it gave me time to pursue an old hobby."

"I saw the little animals you carved. You could probably find a market for them." Ken wiped his mouth with his napkin. "Maybe find an art gallery to display them."

Greg smiled. "Do you really think they're that good?"

Ken nodded. "Yes, I do. But where would you go? The cabin's gone. Besides, Bob owned it."

"I thought about seeing if Bob would sell me the land." Greg rubbed the back of his neck. "Or even find another spot around the lake. I could buy a pre-fab cabin and have it put up."

Ken finished his coffee, stood, and gathered up the trash. "Let's talk about it later, after we have a good sleep. I may have another idea."

Inwardly, Greg grinned. He thought he might have an inkling what Ken was going to suggest, but he didn't want to say anything. It had to come from Ken.

* * *

Greg stretched and yawned. The bed was empty next to him. He opened his eyes.

Ken sat, fully-clothed, at the small table with a notepad and pen.

"What are you doing? Come back to bed."

"Just trying to figure some stuff out." Ken turned and smiled. It was his sexy smile, but there was no promise of a bit of fun. "How about you get dressed and we get some dinner and talk about things?"

Greg swung his legs over the side of the bed, stood, and stretched again. "Okay. I need a shower first." He walked into the bathroom.

About fifteen minutes later, after the warm water had washed the remainder of the sleep away, he walked back into the bedroom, rubbing his hair with a towel. "I hope I can find some clean clothes. I need to do some laundry." He rummaged through the drawer in the dresser. "I also need to do some more shopping. It's surprising how much you need when you lose everything twice in a couple of months."

Ken stood, walked to him, and put his arms around him from behind. "Just think of all the clothes I've had to have over a thousand years."

Greg chuckled. "It must be fun changing styles." He twisted to face Ken. "I can picture you in tights and a tunic." It was a sexy image.

Ken leaned in and kissed him. "I'll have you know I cut a dashing figure in tights and a cod piece."

"Hmmm...cod piece. Do you still have it? That might be sexy to play around with." Greg lay his head against Ken's shoulder, amazed how comfortable it felt. He could stand there holding Ken for hours, it felt that good.

An hour later, they sat across from each other at a nearby steak house. The place was busy with the dinner crowd and Greg wished they'd taken just a little longer getting there, but they'd both been ravenous.

After they placed their orders, Ken opened the conversation, "I've been thinking about what you said about buying Bob's land and rebuilding. I have another idea."

"I'm listening." Greg's pulse raced in anticipation.

"Why not move into my cabin with me?"

Greg cocked his head and grinned. "I thought you said you can't write when I'm around."

Ken ducked his head and looked at Greg sheepishly. "That isn't quite true."

The waiter brought the wine they'd ordered and left.

"Okay. What is quite true?" Greg sipped his wine.

Ken played with the stem of his wine glass. "I didn't want you to know what I am. When I left you, it was so I could morph and exercise my wings."

Greg frowned. "So you weren't writing?"

Ken looked in his eyes. "Yes, I was writing. I was also flying around. But, hear me out." He sipped his wine. "You've never been in my cabin. It's roomier inside than Bob's was. In addition to the loft bedroom, there's also one on the lower floor. I have enough room that I can write in one room, and you can whittle your animals in another."

"And when you want to fly."

Ken grinned. "Then you can fly with me. I'll take you anywhere you want to go."

Greg looked at the table and twiddled with his spoon. It just might work. He was willing to try. Actually it was the kind of change he really wanted in his life. He'd stop being alone all the time with only Casey for company. He was getting used to waking up next to Ken. "I'll tell you what. I'm still going to buy that pre-fab cabin and put it up on Bob's land. We'll give it a try. But if it doesn't work, I'll have options."

Ken placed his hand over Greg's. "You know there is an old Celtic custom. People pledge themselves to each other for a year and a day. At the end of that time, they have the option of walking away, or staying together forever. We've known each other just over a month. When the year comes around, we can decide if we want to stay together, or if we want to go our separate ways."

Greg smiled. "I'll agree to that." He gulped. "Now to tell the captain I'm quitting, and this time it won't be an act."

"That could be hairy."

The waiter brought their meals and Ken cut into his steak. "Do you want me to go with you to tell the captain?"

Greg screwed up his face. "Maybe invisibly?" It would give him a lot more confidence knowing Ken was there with him. He wasn't exactly sure what the captain would do when he made the announcement, but somehow he didn't think he'd take the news well.

Ken nodded. "We can do that."

* * *

That night, Greg lay with his head on Ken's chest and his leg over his thighs. "You said you had a twin sister."

"Yeah. She's in England. She married a human, gave him long life, and they have half a dozen kids, grandkids, and I lost count of how many generations."

"So you can give humans long life? Have you ever tried?"

Ken stroked Greg's hair. "Nope. Not sure it would work for a same-sex relationship the way it does for a straight one."

"Have you ever been tempted?" It was something Greg had never even thought of. He wasn't sure if he'd want to live a long time or not, but if Ken was there, it might be worth any heartache involved. He didn't have any other family. Mike had declared all ties severed six years ago.

"Only once. About eight hundred years ago when I was young."

Greg pulled back and looked at him skeptically. "Young? You were what? About two hundred years old?"

155

"Hey, my father was five hundred when he and my mother met."

Greg resumed his place on Ken's chest. "So who tempted you? A knight in shining armor?"

Ken pulled Greg closer. "Actually, he was a king. It was the end of the twelfth century."

"What happened? Why didn't you try?" Greg was growing to love hearing about Ken's early life. It gave history a very different feel.

Ken sighed. "For several reasons. I talked to my dad. He said it wasn't a good idea to interfere with the reigning family of England. Secondly, he was married."

Greg sat up. "Twelfth century? Are you talking about Richard I of England?"

Ken looked at him with dreamy eyes. "Yeah. He was almost as good in bed as you are?"

Greg lightly punched his arm. "I'll show you 'good in bed'."

* * *

The next morning, Greg's heart pounded hard as he knocked on the door of Wood's office. "Can I talk to you for a minute, Captain?"

"Sure. Come on in. Sit down. I'll be with you in a second."

Greg pulled a chair up to the front of Wood's desk. He couldn't remember being so nervous. He felt like he was saying goodbye to a childhood friend, or close family member, then realized in a way that's exactly what he was doing. A lot of people called policemen the brotherhood of the shield, but Greg knew they were all a big family and he was about to walk away from it.

Wood typed a few words into his computer and then looked at Greg. "I wanted to tell you how good a job you and Ken did. Think we can keep him around?"

Greg gave a short chuckle. "I doubt it." He laid his gun, badge, and an envelope on the captain's desk.

"What's this?" Wood frowned as he studied the small pile.

"I tried to give it to you after they burned my house down and shot Casey." He pursed his lips and shook his head. "That time was an act, but this time I'm really quitting. Jackson's death hit hard, but not as hard as Carter's. Even Hudson's death got to me." He stood, walked to the window looking into the squad room, and rubbed the back of his neck.

"What will you do?" The captain slowly pulled the items across the desk and put them in a drawer.

"Ken and I have talked it over." Greg sat back down. "I'm going to move into his cabin with him."

The captain cocked an eyebrow. "Do you think that's wise?"

"Time will tell." Greg steepled his fingers together. "I'm going to talk to your cousin. I feel it's my fault his cabin burned and I'd like to replace it."

Wood held up his hand. "Don't worry about that. He's already had the insurance adjuster out there and everything's taken care of." He stood and held his hand for Greg to shake. "Keep in touch. If you ever change your mind, we'll be here."

Greg also stood and shook Wood's hand. "Thanks, Captain."

He walked back into the squad room. "Well, guys." He bowed to Whitaker. "And gals, this is goodbye. I'll see you around." He did his best to keep his voice steady as it threatened to crack. Saying his farewells was proving harder than he anticipated.

Whitaker's jaw dropped. "You're leaving? What are you going to do?"

Greg grinned. "I'm going to go live in the woods and whittle little animals." He pulled something out of his pocket and placed it on her desk. "Here's something to remember me by."

Whitaker picked up the tiny carving of a sheltie. "It looks just like Casey." She walked over and kissed his cheek. "Don't be a complete stranger, and tell that handsome dragon of yours he'd better be good to you or I'll sic my friends on him."

"I'm sure he heard you."

She looked around the room. "He's here, isn't he?"

Ken materialized beside her, pulled her close to him, and kissed her cheek. "I'll be back. Maybe even take you on another ride." He paused. "That is if your husband won't get jealous."

She snickered. "He'll probably want a ride also. I know my kids will."

Ken nodded. "That could probably be arranged."

It did Greg good seeing Ken get along so well with the people who were part of his family. His life was changing and he felt good about that. He couldn't wait to see what new adventures Ken would take him on. He doubted his life was going to end up being a quiet time whittling away in the woods, but he could hope. As long as Ken was part of his life, he'd be open for anything, because he knew together, they could get through it.

ABOUT THE AUTHORS

A M BURNS

A.M. has been writing to pass the time since high school. The stories he wrote helped him deal with life. A few years ago, he started sharing those stories with friends who enjoyed them and he has started sending his works out into the world to share with other people. He lives in the mountains with his extremely supportive husband. They have a lot of critters, including dogs, cats, birds, horses, and rabbits. When not writing, A.M. spends a lot of time hiking, trail riding, or just driving in the mountains. Nature provides a lot of inspiration for his work and keeps him writing. He is also an avid photographer and falconer. Don't get him started talking about his birds, because he won't stop for a while.

Web contact info:
Website: www.amburns.com
Twitter: AM_Burns
Facebook: www.facebook.com/authoramburns
Goodreads author page:
www.goodreads.com/author/show/5134598.A_M_Burns
Pintrest: pinterest.com/mystichawker/
Amazon Author Page: www.amazon.com/-/e/B0054EVI6W

Mystichawker Press Author Page:
http://www.mystichawker.com/amburns.html

A T WEAVER

A.T. is a great-grandmother in her 70s who lives with her two cats, Cleo and Kiyah, in downtown Kansas City. She didn't start writing until she was 60. When a friend said he'd like to read a book where, 'the boy gets the boy and they ride off into the sunset', her response was, 'I can do that.' She's never liked to be told what she can or can't do. Even with her bad knees and age, she says, "Don't tell me what I can't do. Let me tell you what I can do."

Web Contact Info:
Blogsite: https://alixtheweaver.wordpress.com/
Email: alixtheweaver@yahoo.com

Facebook: www.facebook.com/alix.t.weaver
www.facebook.com/pages/A-T-Weaver-writer/149528070288
Goodreads:_www.goodreads.com/author/show/2783124.A_T_Weaver
Amazon Author Page:
www.amazon.com/A.-T.-Weaver/e/B00ED0S8XY/

More Books From A.T. Weaver:

After coming out to his family, friends and classmates, the only thing Danny wants is what everyone wants. Someone to love. Someone to spend the rest of his life with. Then he meets Mike who fits the image of the man of his dreams. But Mike has a problem

Mike's been alone since his partner committed suicide two years ago. He's always heard the old adage 'marry the boss's daughter to get ahead'. There's a big problem. How does he tell his boss that not only is he gay, but he just spent the night with the boss's eighteen-year-old son?

Available on Amazon.com

And most other places books are sold.

After seeing his family betrayed and executed during the French Revolution, Marrock De Clarency, an immortal, natural-born shifter, makes his way to the New World. As he moves from place to place across the American wilderness, he finds not only the means to his revenge, but also love. Even as the world progresses around him, he prefers the quiet life in remote areas, away from cities and homesteads.

He gives his heart again and again, each time hoping that this time, he's found his mate. A chance encounter in the woods leaves him wondering, has Fate at last led him to his eternal love?

Available on Amazon.com

And most other places books are sold.

More Books From A.M. Burns:

After his family is killed by thieves, sole survivor Trey McAlister is taken in by a nearby Comanche clan. Trey has a gift for magic and the clan s shaman, Singing Crow, makes him an apprentice. While learning to control his powers, Trey bonds with a young warrior and shape shifter, Gray Talon. When they are sent out on a quest to find the missing daughter of a dragon, they encounter the same bandits who murdered Trey s family, as well as a man made of copper who drives Trey to dig deeper into the magics that created him.

It doesn't take them long to discover a rancher near Cheyenne, Wyoming is plotting to build a workforce of copper men and has captured the dragon s daughter they've been searching for. Trey and Gray Talon must draw on all their knowledge and skills to complete their quest one that grows more complicated, and more dangerous, with each passing day."

From DSP Publishing

Available on Amazon.com

And most other places books are sold.

Bigfoot hunters prowl the forests of Cripple Creek, Colorado. That doesn't sit well with Thom Woodmen-a Bigfoot-albeit the runt of his family. Being the smallest has advantages; Thom, in disguise, gets to attend high school, and he's not expected to accomplish much in life. All that changes when he comes across a distressed human in the forest.

Ben Steele is new to Cripple Creek High School, and after a harrowing experience in the woods near his new home, he quickly falls in with Thom Woodmen and his circle of friends. So what if they like to hang out with nature? Ben's got nothing better to do. Trouble is, Ben can't seem to stay out of it-trouble, that is.

However, in saving young Ben's life, Thom inadvertently kick-starts a bonding process that'll change both their lives forever. With the support of family and friends, Thom learns to accept bonding with the human boy. But with the danger overrunning Cripple Creek lately, Thom may be cut down before he can confess his secret and his love.